Taken by the Alien Bandit
Mated to the Baekex Bandit
Alina Riley

Chapter 1

Astrid

I take a breath, slowly letting it out. It's okay, it should be fine. There's still half a month before rent and payroll are due. There's still time to earn enough from the inn to cover that. I pull out the elastic band that holds my ponytail and rearrange my hair.

My hair is fine; it's well prepared for the day, but I can't stop myself from redoing it. I've done that more times than I can count, but still... My heart races in my chest. There's still a swelling pulse inside me that urges me to do something instead of sitting around.

Around me, the quiet inn sits without giving an answer. I love this place that smells like wood with all the furniture with a nice touch of time and years. This is a warm cozy place away from the cold outside.

At the fireplace, there are cracking noises of cherrywood, waiting for someone to visit. Behind me are barrels of wine and beer for travelers.

I should have known it wasn't a good idea to have an inn here on a distant planet that isn't on any major trading route.

I'm not the one who started it here, though.

At least this place is well-maintained, clean, and tidy for the patrons. I slowly turn around in my spinning chair behind the reception desk. Nobody is here, so maybe this will be another evening with no guests.

The wooden tables and chairs in front of me are empty and quiet. It's getting dark now, so maybe no one wants to come.

This used to be a tourist planet, but no longer.

"Hey, boss." My server boy, Keenya, is there with a towel in his hands. "I cleaned the rooms upstairs."

I nod, forcing a smile. "Good job. Now maybe you can check our stock in the kitchen."

"Sure." He leaves with a bounce in his steps.

He's a bit too happy. Maybe that's the perk of being an employee; they get paid no matter what happens.

I would hate to let this inn fail, but... if nothing is done, that will be inevitable.

The landlord won't be happy if I keep asking for an extension. He knows how hard it will be to get another dummy to rent this place, so maybe that's the only reason he lets me stay here.

To keep losing money on this business.

Edezon is a planet at the edge of several galaxies, between what's called the Empire and the Alliance, two big powers with plenty of planets. Actually, the Alliance is composed of three smaller galaxies coming together for peace. The Empire... Thrizek is the main planet, and they rule over the others with a strong fist.

In theory, Edezon belongs to the Alliance. But there have been rumblings about the Empire looking to expand its influence, like always. Being on the edge, no one cares about this little planet.

From what I've heard from my parents, Edezon used to be close to a busy space station, which was why they built the inn here. But... there was a war, and with the tension, the space station moved, and... now I'm left with this ghost town of a planet.

It's hard for Keeyna to have no idea that we are in trouble. Maybe he just pretends to be happy and doesn't want to cause me extra stress. That's nice of him.

No one is here, so I don't have to serve anyone. I'm the boss here, but I'm also the bartender, the servant, and... the one that's there to pick up whatever mess there is.

If there's no one here, the only mess will be the financial side. It's still me taking care of that.

Maybe I should get my dinner now. Luekotz is meant to be a chef for the guests. But now, he may as well be my personal chef. At least I'm not the one doing the dishes.

I'm about to stand and leave the counter when the bell at the door rings.

My heart skips a beat. What kind of stupid day is this? Even the wind mocks me?

"Here, open?"

Oh, someone is talking. So that's not wind?

Dammit! That means someone is here.

I snap my head up from the counter, trying my best to contain a grin so that I won't scare them. The last thing travelers want is to get robbed, and therefore anything that smells fishy will drive them away.

"Sure, we are open. Grab a seat. You can let me know when you are... ready... to... order..."

The being in front is a big male in a leather jacket. He has horns and yellow scales. He's scowling and he comes straight to the counter.

There are five beings following him: one woman, and the rest of different species. A total of six... Are they here to rob me?

Fuck...

I don't know whether my luck or theirs is bad. I have nothing for them to rob.

The five behind the lead male look around. Four of them stop at a table and sit while the woman follows the leading male. There are so many species that I don't even know what they are called.

That male with golden scales comes right at the counter and plants his hands on top, towering over me with his scary horns. There's a laser gun on his belt. He isn't using it, but... it doesn't mean he has no plan to use it.

"You, the boss?" He has a flat and cold voice, sending a shiver down my spine.

"Yes... How can I help you?"

I've never been robbed before. I suppose I should shout for Luekotz, but there are a lot of them, and they are all armed. We also have weapons, but... they have more hands, and this one is right in my face.

Is it wrong to hope he would destroy some stuff so that I can at least claim insurance and survive the month? Just don't kill me. I don't want to die.

He's about to say something more when the woman arrives. She rests her hand on the male's shoulder. On any other occasions, seeing humans like me among all the other beings is comforting, but when she's a part of these being, I'm not sure how to feel...

She sighs. "Come on, you're scaring her."

The male stops leaning close to me and takes a step back. "Me?"

The woman with golden hair chuckles while she rolls her eyes. "Yes, we know that talking isn't your strong suit. I told you to let me do the talking."

The talking about getting me to hand over the money?

She smiles and gives me a nod. She is also armed. I know most travelers are, but it doesn't make me feel better. I also have a laser gun under the table, but my hands are shaking a bit too much to use it.

"Hello, sorry he scared you. We aren't bad beings." She offers her hand to shake mine. I force myself to do so.

No evil being will say that they are evil.

She continues, "I'm Kimberly and this is Nelutho. We come in peace. He just doesn't know how to make himself look better. Sorry about that. He should know that barging in to places too quickly is bad."

Too quickly? So they want to do this slowly?

She says, "We've been traveling around the nearby planets looking for a group of bandits. Have you seen them? Their leader is a purple male being, that has a tail."

I shake my head. If they are here to warn me about that, they probably aren't bandits. "No, as you can see outside, there's no ships here. No one's here but my workers and me."

Kimberly looks around. I swallow. It feels like I'm shrinking in front of these beings. I wish I could speak highly of this place. I love this inn, but this isn't the best location.

She nods. "Hm... I see. It's good if they aren't here. But you be careful. They can be very dangerous."

"Dangerous as in, they will rob me?"

She scowls. "There are rumors of them burning down villages and murdering everyone. They rob ships and space stations."

"How many are there?"

"We aren't very sure. We think they are a large group and the one we are looking for is a breakout group, probably looking for new pasture."

"Should I report them to the Patrol?"

The male scowls. "No Patrol."

Kimberly squeezes that male's arm. "He means that calling the Patrol may not be the best. You know, they may not be around. I hope they don't come here. But if they do..."

She exchanges a glance with the male. Nelutho, huh? She says, "I'd say... don't try to fight them. Even if they don't come as a whole group."

Nelutho smirks. Kimberly rolls her eyes at him. "Come on, we may not be nearby either. What if she got caught trying to contact us? They wouldn't even blink to kill her and everyone else."

Nelutho sighs. "Well... Don't die."

Kimberly says, "Just be careful. If it's safe, try to contact us. Here is our number." She puts a card on the counter and pushes it to me.

I take it and check. It... is a plain card with only a phone number. There's no name and no title. "Okay. I understand, sir and madam."

Nelutho growls again. "No sir."

Huh?

"I thought you worked for the Empire."

Nelutho hisses. The tension inside him spikes and he lowers his head to show me his horns. That's definitely not a good sign.

I lift my hand between us. "Sorry, the Alliance?"

Kimberly smacks Nelutho's shoulder. "You stop scaring others here and there." After she gives him a pointed look, she turns to me. "We aren't working for anyone. So, no. He doesn't like to be associated with either of those. He's always like that, can't talk like a normal being."

"I'm normal." He straightens with a scowl.

"Fine, fine." She holds his hand. It looks like they aren't just working together as a team of... something. They're closer than that.

I put the card into my pocket. "Okay, so you are bounty hunters."

Nelutho nods. "No work for others."

Well, bounty hunters work for others all the time, unless they aren't successful in getting gigs. Maybe he means that they aren't working for someone at this moment. Or maybe he means that he doesn't work for both the Alliance and the Empire. Like Kimberly said, he doesn't talk normally.

I slowly let out a breath, it looks like they really aren't bad beings. "I understand. Now... do you want to order something? We have beer, food, wine, beds, and rooms."

Nelutho shakes his head, but he soon winces. Kimberly says, "Sure, it's almost dinner time now, we will need some food. Chef's pick for six?"

Nelutho opens his mouth, but he closes it within a blink. Hmm... maybe Kimberly stepped on his toes or something.

Kimberly continues, "And we can each have a beer."

Nelutho shakes his head. "No drinking."

She shrugs. "You are the only one that needs to be on shift, and you don't care about us drinking that much. If you don't want a drink, Drakken will gladly take yours. Just give us six beers."

I nod. It would be great if they order more, as I can use every coin. "Sure, we will have that ready soon. Take a seat."

Kimberly smiles and elbows Nelutho to go with her. Nelutho watches me for another moment before he turns to leave. He makes a step out and he turns at me again. "You be careful."

I nod with my throat tight and bile threatening to rush up my throat. He's... a bit too intimidating. Maybe things would have gone a lot worse if Kimberly wasn't around. And... at any other time, I'd take what he said as a threat. But maybe he's a bit stressed about those bandits and his mood has nothing to do with me. He means well, probably.

I head to the kitchen to tell Luekotz about the order. Chef's special should mean whatever we think is good. It's tempting to give them things I can earn the most from. But...

Maybe they didn't plan to have dinner here.

I glance at the window. Their ship is here. Maybe the plan was to give me a warning and for them to go back to the ship.

Usually, we serve travelers that travel by transport ships. There's a large port fifteen minutes away from here if they drive a small spaceship, which quite some will rent from the port to visit the planet. Most beings with their own spaceships will take a rest here if they got bored with their ship, or they will just eat and then head back to their spaceship to spend the night.

Hm... Maybe I should start charging for parking. But... no one is here, so the fee won't help.

Maybe Kimberly saw that the inn was empty and she pitied me...

I grit my teeth, forcing a smile that is suitable for business when they can see my face, before I head to the kitchen.

I hate it... I should be able to support myself and my workers. But...

Business is business. Regardless of why Kimberly wants to grab food and drink here, I appreciate the business and the coins.

If only...

What should I do to save my business?

Chapter 2

Tlezus

I run my fingers along the box on my hand, which we just got from the poor little cargo ship. It's made of fine wood, with a nice necklace inside that will be worth quite some coins.

There's an urge in my tail. Wild energy makes it tinkle and dance. It's easy to hide my emotion from my face, but my tail is a bit harder.

I nod to Urkaits, my second in command. "Let's get going before the Empire is on our tail."

"Sure, boss." He bows and heads to the command center a door away.

He is also a baekex like me. Being the large and fit-for-combat male that he is, we work to be the most formidable fleet among us. Us, as in the Fleet of baekexes.

We strike terror for the Empire's ships and their associates. Or at least, that's the goal. We live by our own rules — the strongest prevails.

The Empire can think that they have everything in their control. But no, that can't be further from the truth. Rumors are that they have been planning to expand, but the Alliance has been resisting them.

The Empire thinks they can have the whole galaxy they claimed as theirs in their hands, but the Fleet and beings like us shall prove them wrong.

I turn my chair to the window and the screen in front of me, the flashiest thing in the room. I'm the only being here now. My crew is all outside: some are counting the loot, and some are in the command center watching over the operation of the spaceship.

This will make the Empire mad. I smirk as I take a sip of water. I need wine, or some fine faldea. This successful attack deserves fine liquor for my crew.

The Empire can't blame me. If they have worthwhile treasures on the ship, they should have guarded them better. It's their own fault. What I can get is mine.

Now... I scroll out and check the map. We will need a good planet that will let us take a rest and be safe for my crew to enjoy themselves.

We are flying away from the ship we annihilated. It may take some time before the Empire finds out that their cargo is missing. I won't be sorry for the soldiers that died in the fight. If they volunteered for the Empire, they know what's waiting for them.

We didn't kill everyone, though. We know the Empire has control of a lot of planets. It would be great if we could help them, but we can't, not right now. We know many are forced to work for the Empire against their will. So, if they resist, we kill them, and if they don't, we'll leave them alone.

The win is important, but more importantly, the Empire will fear us. The beings shall know where to go and they shall know who's the one trying to help them.

I stretch my arms. It was a good fight. There is heaviness in my limbs, but the nice type, the kind that marks success.

Now, back to looking for a good place to spend the evening. A planet that is probably less frequented and somewhere the Empire won't go. At the same time, a place that will entertain our business.

Hm...

There are a lot of planets on the map, but not all of them would welcome us there.

There is a knock on the door. I call for them to come inside. Olith, my wise counselor, enters.

I stand from my seat. "Olith, how's it going?"

"Captain, we are good. We long for your presence with us."

Ah... "I'm on my way there. What do you think about our mission?"

"It was a success for sure."

I like that. A success.

I head out of the strategic center and he follows. I click the button on the wall with my tail to close the door. "Anything I should have paid attention to? Or, anything for the next mission?"

He chuckles. He's an older baekex with a lot of experience in everything. "Don't get ahead of yourself.

Enjoy the moment. We need to get the money before we worry ourselves with another mission."

"Sure."

I don't care a lot about the money. It's nice to have, enough is good for me and my beings. We take the Empire's things, but we don't always keep everything. The Empire tortures and exploits others for their endless greed, and we swear to keep ourselves away from that.

Olith asks, "Has my captain decided where to go?"

I shake my head. "I'm not sure. We are getting close to the edge of the Empire now, and getting close to the Alliance. I don't know about staying deep into Alliance territory. They know about us, but I don't want to cause them trouble. While we are different, we are the same in more ways than they want to admit."

Olith muses as we turn a corner, but his tail shows nothing. "Indeed. The Alliance is our ally."

The Empire knows we often hide in the Alliance's territory, and they protest and complain often, like the whiny and spoiled brats they are. The Alliance has made statement after statement that they will go after us: the Fleet and groups that are like us. They never follow through, though, at least not while trying their best.

In return, we don't attack the Alliance's associates unless they strike first. A fair deal. Unwritten, but understood by everyone with a brain.

In the command center, my crew is watching the screen, taking note of nearby ships, if there are any, and also a ton of other tasks.

A few see me and stand to greet me, and more follow until they are all standing.

I nod to them. "We have done well. We will go to a suitable planet to rest on, and we shall enjoy ourselves there."

They erupt into cheers, which I enjoy.

But now, I need a planet to land on and not disturb the Alliance too much.

I gesture for my crew to get back to work. Regardless of the destination, we are leaving the Empire's territory first.

I go to my set, which is in the center of the command center, overwatching the beings a few stairs down. Urkaits bows his head as I sit, he's standing next to my seat, also watching the screen.

On the screen, there are shiny dots with different colors for planets with different levels of risk. This ship is the white dot in the center, slowly moving away from those reds and oranges.

"Urkaits, do you have a planet in mind?"

"Yes, Captain. Edezon. It's supposed to be the Alliance's planet, but it's on the edge. You know the Empire thinks that everything's theirs, so the Alliance doesn't have much there. At the same time, the Empire still has a plan to overtake the Alliance and won't want to stir trouble this early."

I tap my fingers on the control panel right in front of me. A distant planet no one wants to care about sounds like a good idea.

"The planet itself?"

"Was a tourist spot, but after the space station that used to be there moved away to avoid being the sandwich between the two forces, it's kind of dead."

So that means not many beings will be there, not bad.

I nod, looking at Olith. He also nods.
I say, "Edezon that is."

Chapter 3

Astrid

I stare into the sky as Eeldeir is setting, painting the sky a purple-orange. Nelutho and his crew spent the night in their own ship and left in the morning after they had breakfast at my inn.

I still think that it is because Kimberly wanted to give me some business, but money is money.

Will I be lucky again today? Yesterday was a good moral boost, but I need business to be consistent before the inn can stay. I have already posted a bit more on the inn's site on the Linksys, so hopefully that will result in some travelers wanting to visit this planet.

Maybe I'm biased, but the sky is great at dawn and now, between the afternoon and the evening.

In front of me, far far away, close to the horizon, there are mountains. Most of them are rocky mountains.

I don't know much about mountains and terrains, but there ought to be some scenery that's worth visiting.

The empty parking lot stares back at me. Staying outside and looking at the sky will soon be a killer more than a help for my mood. Maybe I should wait inside the inn and see what other promotional material I can come up with.

I avoid looking at the empty tables and head straight to the counter, picking up my tablet and turning to stare at the beer barrels.

Better than the otherwise empty inn.

I am about to switch on my table when the bell at the door rings. Hm… is that Luekotz? I don't remember if he went outside, but maybe he did.

"Hey, is this place open?" The voice belongs to a male that's definitely not Luekotz.

I turn around. "Sure, welcome—"

Fuck… is this a purple male? And a tail? And… there are two more purple males following him. The leading one has a drop-dead handsome face with a sharp jawline and blond hair. He's wearing a grey robe with a hood. The robe doesn't hide the guns he hangs on his belt and the other devices that are also there, which I doubt mean anything good. These must be the bandits I was warned about yesterday.

He lifts his brows at me. "Huh? Something wrong?"

I shake my head. He better never find out that I know who he is. "Nothing's wrong. Most of our patrons arrive a bit earlier in the day, so I'm a bit surprised."

"Ah, okay." He doesn't seem to see me shaking while I made things up, which is great. From what Nelutho said, this is a space bandit and his group is dangerous…

He looks around. "Hm… this place looks empty."

A stream of heat burns my cheek. I hate this. "I guess that means we can provide even more personalized service for you and your group."

He smirks. His tail moves some more. It's also purple like the rest of him, but the tip of the tail is a light brown, like a rattlesnake's, with thicker bands on it. "I like how that sounds. If there are no others here, it'll be for the best."

There is a glimpse of something that screams danger in his eyes. My heart skips a beat. Maybe Nelutho shouldn't have come yesterday. Maybe it would be a lot easier not knowing who these beings are.

I nod. "Glad you like it. Does your group plan to stay here for the night? Or on your ship? I can get the staff to start preparing the rooms now if you like."

He taps his fingers on his cheek as he watches me, seemingly considering his options. His fingers look like mine, but they look rougher, and he has some sharp nails that seem like claws. "What do you have for my crew?"

"Huh? Beer? Wine? Music?"

He frowns. "That's all?"

I swallow. What does he want?

He muses, "That's not very interesting. You see, my males want to have some fun."

Ah… I know now. He wants us to have some pleasure workers for his crew. No, there are none of those here. I'm barely paying rent and payroll for the limited hands I have. I don't have the extra money to keep any pleasure workers around.

But I want his business, even if they are notorious bandits.

I clear my throat. "We don't have anything like that, but we have funny stand-up comedy here."

"Eh?"

"Jokes. We also have magic tricks."

"Magic tricks. Come on, we aren't kids."

And those aren't regular programs either. I can only hope Keeyna can pull it off and be funny enough.

I shrug. "I know. Which part of you looks like a kid anyway? I'm not offering you child play, for sure. Why would I waste your time? That's not how I conduct business here. But if you have no interest in that, it's okay. I understand not all beings have good taste."

He growls. I try my best to not shake under his gaze that threatens to tear me into pieces. He smirks. "Now you're insulting my taste; that's pretty brave. Fine, my beings will stay here for the night. There are twenty of us. Some will stay on the ship, but get us twenty rooms."

That will fill more than half of the rooms, nice.

"Sure. Want some drinks or food to kick it off? I suppose you're having a celebration or something?"

He lifts my chin with his finger. His claw tickles. His eyes darken as he watches me right in the eyes. "Hm... You seem to know something."

I... "I'm observant. I run this inn. We serve a lot of patrons. I know a thing or two."

He tilts his head to the side. His tail wriggles some, which I hope doesn't mean anything bad. "Interesting. Faldea?"

Ah, he knows about wine. "Sure, we have that. How much?"

"Hm, then this place is at least decent. Don't care, my crew is here to enjoy the night, so until they have enough."

I silently suck in a breath. That... could mean big money for me.

"No cap at all?"

He shakes his head. "No, as much as they want. If you run out, give them beer."

This is crazy talk. I stare at him for longer than it will be polite.

He lifts an eyebrow. "What, you don't think I can pay for it?"

"It's not about that." Except yes, especially since I know their occupation. Maybe Nelutho's warning is a bit useful here. But these are bandits, so...

He snorts. "I can pay you in coins, no card." He turns around to his beings that are seating themselves already. "Urkaits!"

Another big and hulky purple being comes over with a backpack in his hand. "Captain, here you go."

The captain takes it and put it on the counter. He opens the zipper and there reveals... a large pile of coins, more than I have ever seen.

Before I can take one to check, he closes the edge of the backpack. I blink.

He smirks. "Now you know I have the money."

"You won't even let me check one?" I take a shaky breath. I know these are bandits and this is dirty money, but the landlord probably won't care where I get the money. Not to mention, I don't know these beings, so I can play the victim if necessary. "Not to doubt you, but you know there are bad beings out there using fake stuff."

He leans close to me. "You're interesting, but I guess if I want faldea, I can't blame you for being cautious. Check all you want."

I reach for the backpack and pick up a coin from deep inside it. It has the right weight and the carvings of the Empire look like the real thing. "There are all Thrizek coins?"

"Most of it. I think there are some from planets in the Alliance, but not many."

I toss the coin back into the backpack. "I will trust you. Does your crew also want food? Or just faldea? Sounds a bit boring, even though that's an amazing wine."

He licks his lips. "What kind of snacks do you have?"

"Crispy bacon and sausage rolls? Fried chicken? Crackers?"

He squints. "Human food, huh?"

I shrug. "Most travelers like to try something new. Or tell me what you want and we can have our chef make it?"

I earn a decent profit from special orders compared to our regular menu. He's so rich that he probably wouldn't care anyway. Not that I dare scam a group of bandits. But it isn't a scam if I just upsell them on snacks.

He muses. "I will give those a try. I don't visit a lot of places run by humans."

"I know, we are pretty rare in the galaxy."

There's a flash in his eyes. My throat tightens. Saying that out loud doesn't seem like a good idea, now more than ever.

There're only three of us here in the inn, and there are twenty purple beings in the bandit crew. On this remote planet... we could disappear without a trace and no one would ever find out...

Rare... may sound like honey for bandits. I can only hope this group isn't interested in selling beings.

He nods. "Yes, humans are pretty rare. I hope you have good food, otherwise, I'll ask for a refund."

It looks like he's in a good mood, definitely here to celebrate. If that's the case, maybe I can stroke his ego or joke with him. "If it's in your stomach, it'll be hard to refund it."

He chuckles. "Get me the food, human." He walks off to the tables to join his crew, who are already chatting with their voices echoing throughout the whole inn.

I turn on the music for them. I'm going to do whatever I can to get them to drink more. These are very strong and large beings, but I don't even remember what his specie is called.

They are busy chatting, so maybe I should take the chance and let Nelutho know about them.

If Nelutho comes... they will fight here, and that will break things and I will get insurance money. But there won't be wine and snacks and room money.

Hmm... sounds like profit is better.

I go into the kitchen where Keeyna and Luekotz are both there. There are frowns on their faces.

Keeyna asks, "Are those the ones we are warned about?"

I glance at the outside. They are busy chatting and the music will drown out my voice. "We have to act good.

They have money and they are ready to get wine and food. Put up a good show. They don't know we know."

The two of them glace at each other with deep frowns.

I pat their shoulders. "Come on. It isn't like we can flee now. For better or worse, we have to keep them happy."

Keeyna nods. "I understand. But… they aren't our usual patrons. What should we do?"

I gently squeeze his shoulder. "You will go entertain them with some jokes and your magic tricks."

"Huh?" He stares at me. "I know I'm kind of funny, but…"

"You can do it."

I turn to Luekotz. "Get them faldea. We will get them to drink a lot, and then they fall asleep. By tomorrow, they will all be gone. We will have the money and that will solve quite a lot of our problems."

Keenya takes a breath. "Okay, I will try my best. Maybe they won't be dangerous when they're drunk."

"Yes, that's the plan." Maybe I'm bad for coaxing him and taking advantage of how he's a bit younger and has little experience with things, but… like I said, we don't have a lot of choices.

Luekotz straightens. "Other than faldea, what do they want?"

"Crispy bacon and sausage roll, fried chicken, Crackers. Human food."

He lifts an eyebrow. "Really? Fried chicken with faldea?"

I shrug. "Give them something else until they get a bit drunker then."

He sighs. "I understand we need to sustain this inn, but that's not the best choice with faldea. I think that works with beer, but anyway... Maybe baekexes will like that combination."

Oh, right, baekex is their species name. Purple with a tail.

I nod to them. "Let's try our best, team." I glance at the outside. "And be quick, before they think that we're calling for help."

Chapter 4

Astrid

I lift my mug and toast with the baekexes near me. Now, I'm sitting at their table, doing rounds and keeping them entertained.

Quite a few of them are laughing at Keeyna's jokes, jokes that I have heard more times than I can count. Most of them are boring quotes from cartoons and movies, human stuff. But maybe everything is new to these purple beings and they find them funny. Nice.

Something wraps around my waist and pulls me to the side of the chair. Their leader smirks at me. I gasp, trying to be subtle with it. His body is warm as he pulls me close to him until my body is pressed against his.

He lifts my chin with a hand while he takes a sip of his drink. The thing that holds me to him is still on my waist. Is that... his tail?

My heart skips a beat when he looks at me with those intense eyes. What does he want? Is he drunk already?

He sets down the mug. "I've never seen a human this closely." He rests his hand on my cheek. I shiver from his touch and he laughs. "Are you scared of me?"

The rest of the baekexes laugh. My cheek is burning as they all stare at me as if I'm something special.

Their leader's tail, especially the tip, rubs my side. He's waiting for my response, and he looks like he's enjoying my flustered look. Maybe I should put up my good act.

"Well, all of you are such large males, it's hard to not worry some."

The leader's grin grows. "Worry about what? You think we'll eat you alive?"

Now his hand is on my thigh. My body is burning hot from his touch. I rest a hand on his chest, leaning closer to him. Maybe he's never been close to a human, but I've also never been close to a baekex.

He's larger and taller than me. When I lean onto him, my cheek ends up on his chest, close to his shoulder. "Oh, I bet you could eat me well. And if I'm not alive, what's the purpose?"

As far as I know, baekex don't eat humans and don't eat other beings, so...

He laughs and takes another gulp of his drink. "You want me to eat you out? Naughty human. Be careful of what you're asking for."

I slide my hand down his chest. I flinch when... his cock is already hard and... large. I know he mentioned wanting some pleasure workers for his crew. So... is he going to make me his pleasure worker for the night?

Will that result in extra tips?

He asks, "What? Like what you're stroking?"

The table erupts into roars. There is fire in the other baekex's eyes. They for sure know what their captain is talking about.

Now... I'm not sure if baekexes are into... sharing.

The leader hisses and sneers, the others stop their growls, which quickly turn into murmurs.

He says, "We'll find a place to get pleasure. Tonight, we'll drink." He lifts the mug, but soon snarls. "Where's the kid? Refill my mug!"

While Keenya hurries and scrambles, I stroke his cock. He's even larger and harder now. He lets out a low growl and his cock twitches under my hand. Hopefully, he will forget about his empty mug for a bit longer.

He... He's huge. How will he feel inside me? Can he fit into me?

From the snarl and hiss, he won't share me with the other males, but he's definitely going to put me in his bed for the night.

Maybe... maybe I won't complain too much. His size is promising. But still, he better tip me extra.

He hums. "You are a naughty female human. Hm... Is there a way to say that without that extra words?"

I chuckle. "Try woman."

"Good, naughty woman."

I peck a kiss on his cheek and rub him harder. I whisper in his ear, "You're hard to resist."

His cock twitches under my hand and his breath halts for a moment. Hopefully, I haven't overdone it and he won't think that I'm trying to get him in some way.

His tail lets go of my waist and it sneaks between my legs. I'm in a pair of jeans, so it isn't like he can directly rub my pussy, but... the thicker bands on the tip of his tail tease me. He has a thick tail that could... dammit.... Maybe I'm the crazy one thinking that he will fuck me with his tail.

Keeyna is back with another jar of feldea, pouring it for the leader and the other baekexes around the table. He glances at me, and there's a faint shade of red on his face.

I swallow with heat swirling in my stomach. Keenya is younger, but he isn't a kid, so... But maybe I'm not who he thought I was when I'm here wrapped in this purple being's arms and flirting with him. At least Keenya can't see what's happening under the table from where he stands.

Keenya blinks when he catches my gaze. He quickly leaves for another table.

Maybe I should feel bad for trying to make these beings pay us more with this flirting and my probably predictable nighttime event. But...

The leader lets out a low growl when my hand stops. His tail presses into my jeans, cooler, but as a threat, that's enough to keep me working on his cock. His trousers may burst.

He stands, almost pulling me with him. "Baekex warriors, enjoy our victory. We shall celebrate this evening. I will meet you all tomorrow."

Ah, now he decides that instead of teasing me or letting me tease him here, he's going to put me on his bed.

His crew stands and toasts with him. I wink to Keenya who is serving them a new round of snacks while busy entertaining them with jokes. I hope he remembers to get them to drink more, so they fall asleep and skip over the phase when drunk beings break things.

The leader gestures for me to go with him. I stand and follow, trying my best to ignore how wet I am and hoping the thick fabric of my jeans isn't soaked with visible wet marks.

His tail dangles in front of me as he walks with his hands in his pockets. Maybe he's secretly hoping that he can hide his erection like that.

We arrive at the stairs at the corner of the inn. He stops. "Lead the way."

"Sure." I take a step in front of him and walk upstairs. "How far do you need me to lead you along?"

He grunts. "Or lead me on?"

I shrug. "I didn't start that. Your tail started that."

"Oh, my tail. You just can't wait to see what's going to happen."

"Are you the type that will overpromise?"

He laughs. "I like this. I'm going to overdeliver until you can't take me anymore."

Dammit... he sure knows how to dirty talk.

We arrive at the last room in the corridor. I pull out the keys. "Do you like this room? I think you will like this one. Or do you want one that's closer to the stairs? This one is larger, though."

He shrugs. When the corridors upstairs are dimmer, his eyes are almost glowing yellow. "More important is a bigger bed."

"Ah, I knew this would be the right room for you." I insert the key. My hands are shaking. "You're going to like this."

A stream of heat presses up to me, and something hot presses on my ass. His arms wrap around me and he grinds his hardness on me. "And you are going to love me so much that you can't stop begging me for more."

My heart races so much that it may jump out of my throat. With that size, he isn't joking.

Chapter 5

Astrid

As soon as the door opens, he sweeps me off my feet into a bridal carry. I yelp and almost drop my key. He stares at it for a second. "Don't tell me you have to go downstairs to open the doors for the rest of them."

I shake my head. "There is another set of keys down there for my staff."

He grins. "Smart." He heads into the room, closing the door with his tail. "I like that bed. Looks like you can squirm and it won't collapse that easily."

Fuck...

He puts me on the bed and wastes no time. He yanks at my jeans; I unbutton them quickly before he can break them. I don't have that much extra money to get myself new clothes.

I reach for the buckle of his belt when his tail wraps my hands. He smirks. "In a hurry?"

Dammit! He doesn't think I'm trying to reach for his guns, right?

I swallow. "You are such a tease. Come on. Otherwise, I'd hope you brought spare trousers for yourself."

He laughs. "Interesting. Are all women like you? So horny without a horn?"

"Well, no idea. I'm not interested in other women, so..."

He swears under his breath. Maybe it's in his own language, but that... stirs a storm inside me. He takes off his belt and tosses it to the side along with his weapons. There isn't much for him to worry about when I'm a smaller female than him by quite a lot.

He yanks off my jeans along with my panties in one go.

I chuckle and lift my legs, making it easier for him to get them off me completely. "Are you going to mount me like a beast now?"

"Tempting."

Now that he doesn't have weapons on his waist, I reach for his trousers and sneak my hand under them. His cock throbs under my hand as I free it. His cock is purple like the rest of him, with his tip an even darker shade of purple.

I wrap his cock with both of my hands. It's so huge. Will he fit inside me without breaking me in half?

He picks up my legs, putting them on his shoulder, leaving me wide open for his hungry and lust-filled eyes. "A human pussy."

His cock is right in front of my entrance, teasing and mocking me with his heat that's almost there. He presses a finger onto my clit, sending a spark down my spine.

He starts slow, as if he's figuring out my clit and my body. It's so slow that it hurts. My pussy contracts and I am getting wetter from every rub.

I gasp. He's going to toast me with the tease. I ask, "What's your name?"

He snickers. "So curious?"

"Well, if you can't make me scream your name regardless, you can keep it to yourself."

His cock jerks and touches my entrance. Fuck!

"Tlezus."

"I'm Astrid."

Um... is this a time for self introduction though?

"Astrid, sounds nice."

"Thanks." What else should I say?

This may be the silliest thing ever. When he had me on his shoulder, my ass off the bed, and his cock right at my entrance, all I did is to ask him his name.

His finger rubs my pussy harder now. "So wet, so ready for my cock."

Before I can say a thing, he pushes his finger into my pussy. All the words I want to say warp into a moan.

He chuckles, slowly making his way in. His thick finger stretches my wall, rubbing against my folds.

His finger moves in and out of me, still testing to see how he can play with my body. I arch and move, needing more from him.

He says, "You're getting impatient now, can't wait to get fucked."

"If you can't make it good, just let me go now."

He growls, pulls his finger out of me, and before the emptiness can sink in, his cock slams right into me.

I yelp when his huge tip stretches me, even more than his finger can prepare me for. His rough cock rubs my wall hard, but the pain is soon replaced by mind-numbing pleasure. I have never taken a huge monster of a cock before. This is so amazing.

He pulls out some before plunging in even deeper. "Hm... so tight."

He pins into the deepest part of me, with plenty of his cock still outside of me. His cock throbs and grows larger, filling out every inch of me.

I gasp when the fullness becomes overwhelming. "You are going to destroy me."

"Do you want that?"

I grit my teeth when he starts moving inside me, pumping in pleasure. Every thrust makes me more of a whore, craving his large baekex cock.

It doesn't take long before I'm rocking my ass, matching the rhythm of his thrusts.

He grabs my boobs, his fingers flicking my nipples. "So women have these sensitive nibs."

"Mmm... Yes! More!"

"Beg harder."

"Tlezus! Fuck me like I'm a whore. I want your hard cock."

"Such a helpless female."

"Yes! Don't stop fucking my helpless pussy."

He laughs. When he pinches my nipples, an orgasm explodes through me.

He groans when my juice spills out around his cock. "What does this mean?"

I grimace. Is that even a question? I hate how easy it is for him to fuck me until I squirt.

He licks his lips, and soon, the fire of lust lights up in his eyes. "Interesting body."

My walls grab tighter onto him, needing even more from him. I was planning to let him use my body for my own benefit, but maybe... this is going to turn into more benefit for me.

He pulls his cock out of me. I scream. He can't do that to me. When only his tip is left in me, he slams all the way in.

"Tlezus! Arrh!"

"Be a good slut."

He starts pounding my pussy, so hard and fast that orgasms wreck through my body. The bed squeaks and the room is filled to the brim with the dirty noises his monster makes with my hungry pussy.

This is the leader of a group of bandits who I should report. But for now, I let him thrust his cock into me, dominating all my senses, and making my pussy his.

How did this happen? Am I really that much of a slut?

I thought I was trying to rile him up and tease him, but now... I just need him to bang me hard and show me how much I craved a great, huge cock.

I moan when another high hits me. I'm whimpering and shaking, but he isn't slowing down at all. Maybe baekexes have a lot more stamina and are good to ravish me.

"Tlezus! Yes!"

"Such a slut."

"Make me your whore. Come inside me."

He snickers, his fingers digging into my ass, and his claws hurt, almost breaking my skin. The pain merges with the pleasure from his cock, making it even stronger and harder to resist. "You don't get to make the call."

The darkness and the husky words burn me. My toes curl, letting another wave of pleasure wash over me.

"Why?" I scream when he pulls from me. I'm so close to another release! "Oof!"

Something else thrust into my pussy, moving in and out of me quickly. That's not as thick, not burning hot, but...

I stare behind me to find his tail buried into my pussy. He has a grin on his deadly handsome face, enjoying my reaction. The bands on his tail tickle and rub me well.

He says, "Be patient. Like I said, you are going to crave me, to beg for more. And soon, you'll touch yourself and finger your pussy, burning in lust for my cock, which you won't get."

Is that referring to how he's only staying here for a night? I want to laugh at how silly that sounds, but if this keeps going, if he keeps pounding my pussy...

His tail leaves my pussy, making my walls clench onto nothing. I'm about to swear and squirm when his tail moves to my ass, the tip searching for the entrance from behind me.

I gasp when his tail parts the cheeks of my ass. He's that close to thrusting into me, also taking my ass for himself.

He rubs my clit. "Relax. It's going to hurt, but you will love it."

Maybe that's why he fucked me with his tail. He's going to use my juice to lubricate my hole for himself...

The heat in my stomach grows, spreading to the rest of my body. I may catch fire at any time.

Before I can blink, his cock rams into my pussy again. I scream as my body hurries to prepare for him.

When his cock rubs my wall, pulling my attention away, his tail penetrates my ass.

I grab a handful of the bedsheet, my body shaking from the pain from behind. He's too large, this won't work.

He moans with his eyes close. "Hm... that hole is even tighter. Just relax."

I try, but I can't. His tail is a bit too thick and those bands on it are... maybe they are designed to fuck my ass...

He slides in and out of my tight hole. His cock also moves inside me, slowly working up the pleasure.

I moan when his tail pushes deeper into me. Maybe he will break me, but maybe it will be so good that I won't mind.

A new heat rises inside me, something that I have never experienced before. His tail and his cock are both slamming and pounding me. Both my holes are used to the maximum, devoured by this baekex that leads a deadly group of bandits.

His cock feels even larger when my ass is filled by his tail. I must really look like a slut now with both my holes filled. When I arch and move, I'm helping him dominate my body.

Outside of the room, in the corridors, I can hear voices. Maybe the other baekexes are done drinking and are ready to sleep now.

Tlezus smirks and picks up speed. I can't help but moan like a maniac. He must want that, want everyone to know how he has made me his whore, made me crave him, and made my body his.

Shame burns inside me. I'm so bad for enjoying this. But he's so good at using me, even though this is probably the first time he's touched a human woman.

What has he done to me? His huge cock in my pussy feels right, instead of how he should have broken me with that.

"Good pussy and great ass. So fucking tight." His cock twitches and he picks up speed. "So good that I can do this."

He grabs my boobs, planting his feet by my body as he gets into position to pound my holes hard. "You wanted me to mount you like a beast, huh? Now you get what you asked for."

"Arrh!" The pleasure that comes crashing in is a bit too much.

He shoves me through the clouds, so much so that everything around me ceases to exist.

"Tlezus! Yes! Fuck me!"

"Good, I love how you scream my name. Scream harder."

"Yes!" I do as he said when he takes me even harder. I'm coming hard, as he commands me to.

My body is a mush, his hands on my boobs is the only reason I'm still upright, still kneeling on the bed, into position for him to devour.

His cock twitches inside me and grows even harder. "Now, time to fill this slutty ass."

I scream as his cock explodes inside me. His hot cum fills me and drips out of me. His tail moves even faster inside my ass, ramping up the pleasure until he will crush me with it.

When he pulls out of me, I collapse onto the bed. My limbs and my whole body are pretty much useless now.

He grins, his cock is still half-hard and it looks like he could fuck me again, and maybe again and again.

He lifts my chin. "Looks like you're pretty much done now."

I'm still gasping and panting, my pussy still contracting hard. The orgasms still burn inside me. "You aren't done..."

He winks. "If I want to, I can fuck you the whole day and night."

I... I don't doubt that. His purple cock is shiny with my juice, and also his tail. My cheek burns hotter when I can't pull my eyes from his cock.

He says, "You can't stop looking at me."

Who am I fooling?

I shrug. "Well, you did deliver more than you promised."

"I can do more, but look at you." He leans closer and kisses the tip of my nose. "Sometimes, even one pleasure worker can't handle me. But you are a lot more... may I say, pure? Precious? I won't break you, don't worry."

My heart flutters. Does he mean he can fuck two females at once? I... I mean... I know he can pay for that and if he has the coins, those pleasure workers will please him and let him do whatever he wants to them. But dammit... that's crazy.

He strokes my cheek. "You are burning hot like a cute aovaz now."

I shiver. This is a bit too much. I... may die.

He blinks. "Hm... you should rest."

He joins me on the bed, pulling the blanket up to cover us, and wraps his arms around me. His tail wraps around my legs. Is he worried that I'll flee? Where am I going anyway? This is my inn; I'm not going anywhere.

His warmth wraps around me, so much so that I doubt I will get any sleep. He moves his hand behind my head, nudging me to rest my head against him.

My heart is racing when I do as he wants. Other than the rough pounding, which I loved, he is... gentler than I expected, given what I know about him.

I rest my hand on his abs and he smirks. "Like what you feel?"

This male is a ball of stamina and strength. So very hard to resist. I don't even know whether I want to resist his charm.

This is just a one-night thing, anyway. As long he doesn't hurt my employees or me, all is good.

Chapter 6

Tlezus

Maybe this little inn doesn't have any pleasure workers for my crew, but I have this cute little human female in my arms, with a pussy that's so amazing.

Even the memory of it sends my cock twitching. Hm... It would be so fun if I can keep her. She isn't a pleasure worker, which means I could take her with me if I want to.

In this inn, there are only two other males. I watched when I was still drinking with my crew. There is a kzopto with a large and strong horn, a muscular and tough male. But that's only one kzopto, while my crew far outnumbers him.

Maybe he was hired as a bouncer in case some drunk beings cause trouble. I don't doubt that he could handle a few drunk beings. But my warriors are well-trained to fight; he won't stand a chance against us.

He's just an employee, anyway; there's no way he will fight to his death for this inn. If he's smart, he will pretend he can't see us and let me take this female.

I'm going to put her in my room and fuck her every night.

I lick my lips. That sounds like a plan. I take what I want.

There was another male as well, but he's a tiny one only good to fill my mug with wine and crack some silly jokes. He isn't even a threat.

The woman is fast asleep now. She has cute and soft beige skin. I don't understand how her pussy feels so good, so right for me. Is that a female-human thing? Or... hm... women thing? Or is that just her? She's just that amazing and talented in taking my cock and my tail?

But this woman is probably one of the Alliance's. So, I shouldn't take her without a good reason. I don't want the Alliance to come after me and the Fleet. We don't kidnap innocent civilians.

Wait...

I let go of her. There is a very low vibration from the bed, but it isn't her and it isn't me. There is someone walking somewhere in the inn. No mild vibration can escape a baekex like me. Even though I fucked her till late, I'm up and ready to feel the shakiness.

Astrid is fast asleep. From what I've known, humans aren't the most alert ones. Their senses don't even remotely match my kind.

Is it the kid walking outside, or the chef? I didn't think employees would work that late into the night. But the inn is theirs, so I guess there are no rules that they can't walk around in their inn.

But...

I sit up on the bed, putting my tail on the wall.

Hmm... something isn't right. There seems to be more than one being moving.

Two...?

I hop off the bed and get dressed. Something doesn't feel right.

There is a shout in the corridor from my crew.

Fuck...!

I dress. The heaviness from the sex and the alcohol earlier are all gone. I'm ready to fight no matter when and where.

There are rapid knocks on the door. "Captain, wake up! Someone is coming for us."

I growl. "I'm coming."

Before he can open the door, I open it myself. I'm full-geared, not a leader that will sleep like he's dead.

"Who is it?"

"No idea. Maybe they are bounty hunters. They aren't in the Empire's uniform."

Fuck bounty hunters. They are hired guns that have no backbone and bend for money.

Or... maybe they're the Empire's beings. They're just pretending not to be so that they can attack me in the Alliance's region. No one has a complete list of who's from the Empire and who's not, after all.

I ask, "Urkaits?"

"He's fighting already, Captain."

"Good, I will get there soon."

The male hurries down the corridor to join the fight. I turn into the bedroom. Astrid has woken up.

I lift my brows at her. "How much did you hear?"

"Someone is... attacking?"

Ah... It must be her. The reason we're getting attacked.

"Dress."

She stares at me as if she doesn't understand me. I'm taking her with me now. She thinks that she can get my crew drunk and call the bounty hunters or the Empire with no consequence?

I pull my gun and point it at her. "You heard me."

She tosses the blanket to the side and grabs her clothes that are scattered on the floor.

I move close to the door, pointing another gun at the corridor, just in case.

"I... don't shoot." Her voice is trembling. Something about that makes my cock hard. But I don't need that now. If I find a hint of her selling out my crew, she will be dead.

No, she will have it worse than dead, and after that, she will die a slow and painful death that she will know is her fault.

I take another step into the corridor. There are shouts and laser guns down there already. My crew will fight until I can get away safely. I'm not risking their lives.

I go to catch her. She whimpers and moves away from me. But before she can run, I grab her and toss her over my shoulder.

"Put me down!" She punches my back, but that doesn't last when my tail wraps around her wrists, locking them together.

I spank her ass, and she moans. Dammit, she's such a slut. Or maybe I've broken her.

With my cock and my tail, not bad.

"Shut up and behave, otherwise..."

She shivers but says nothing. Maybe she learned her lesson.

I hurry down the corridor to the stairs. The tables down there are flipped over, and my crew is shooting from behind the barriers. I dash down the stairs before I become a target for them to shoot at.

The kzopto and the kid aren't around. Maybe they're scared of a fight like this. Or... they are with those attacking us. I growl and join my crew.

"Let's get going." I shoot at the attackers while we push the tables forward.

Something moves at the side when I go past the kitchen. The kzopto points at me with his gun. "Put her down."

I snort a laugh. "You're surprised? You called them here."

He shakes his head. "No, we're also surprised. Put her down."

I point my gun at him. "If I were you, I'd hide."

Something from the side jolts. I turn and fire, barely missing the kid and he kicks my stomach. I laugh when he doesn't even move me an inch.

I elbow him and he drops to the floor. "Maybe you don't want to live."

"Keeyna!" Astrid screams and starts kicking and trying to snap out of my hold. "Don't hurt him. I'll go with you, spare them. I'm the boss here and I'm the one who called the hunters here."

What the actual fuck.

I growl, "Really?"

The two inn workers stare at her with horror in their eyes.

Astrid is over my shoulder and she can't see what I'm seeing in front of me, but maybe she can guess. "You heard me. If you want to get mad at someone, it should be me. Don't hurt them!"

I snarl. I don't care about these two anyway. My cock twitches at the thought. Maybe that will be interesting. Now she's rightfully mine after she did that stupid thing.

I still point my gun at those two. "Get inside the kitchen and stop thinking you can be a hero."

That kzopto sneers at me, but he grabs the kid and does as I said. Maybe he isn't that dumb after all.

I turn to the exit, which my crew has already cleared. Whoever's trying to hit us is too weak.

Outside the inn, our ship is intact, and my crew is driving away the last of the forces attacking us. They flee quicker than they come. We are baekexes; those stupid beings are out of their league.

I board my ship with Astrid on my shoulder. This woman dared to hurt us.

There's a fire burning inside me. I will tear her into pieces and she will regret her existence.

Inside the command center, my crew is busy counting to make sure everyone is back on the ship, including the injured.

I toss her to the ground, my tail tugging her head so her ass lands first. "What do you have to say for yourself?"

She shivers, shaking as if I will have mercy on her. I have no mercy on whoever dares to betray me or the Fleet.

The ship starts and lifts from the ground. So much for her silly little inn. If I had more time, I'd burn that place to the ground.

I hiss at her. "Talk to me."

She takes a breath, glancing at the window. We are in space now, and there's nowhere she can flee from us.

She opens her mouth. "You know I didn't call anyone."

I tilt my head to the side. Now, is she playing dumb with me?

"Do you think I've forgotten what you've said?"

She shakes her head. "I was with you all the time. If I had called anyone, you would have found out."

I growl. Does she think I'm that dumb? And she has to say that when all the crew in the command center can hear her?

"Someone had to have outed us."

"Or they have been chasing and following you. Why would I out you? Who are you? Why are those coming after you?"

I snicker. She lied. I know it in her eyes. She knows what we are. "You told them."

She shakes her head. "No, I didn't."

"I'm not going to trust you." My tail wraps around her neck and lifts her. I grab her boobs and feel for anything on her. If I find a phone or something on her, she's done screwed up and I'm going to punish her.

Her boobs are so soft and... hm... now I can't shake how she moaned and screamed my name from my mind, dammit. I squeeze her another time before I move my hands down her body. She shivers and tenses when I go all the way down her body.

I shove my hand between her thighs. To be honest, that has little to do with the search, but to torment her. I have never done something really terrible to a female.

I'm not that kind of male. But if there's a good reason... Hm... Maybe...

She shakes and a low moan escapes her lips. Maybe she likes how my crew can see her squirming on the floor in my hand once they turn around. Maybe that's turning her on. Such a naughty and horny woman.

I move to her pocket. There's... something in it.

I pull that out of her pocket, that's a card with a string of number on it. She gasps. Maybe that's what this is. A number to call the Empire's force.

"Urkaits."

"Yes, Captain."

I hand him the card. "Check whose number is that."

She's shaking now. If she dares to out me, she should know about the consequence. I run my finger down her throat. "Tell me. How much did they pay you?"

"No, it's not about that."

"Then why? The Empire has someone you love?" My gut twists. Is that the case? I know that's something the Empire does, but usually to those they send to govern other planets, keeping some of the loved ones so those won't dare to go against them.

I would hate to hurt her for that.

She shakes her head again. Her lips tremble, but she says nothing. I pat her other pocket and pull out a phone. "Urkaits, also check this."

"Sure, Captain."

I straighten and leave her on the floor. She balls herself up, watching me with horror in her eyes. There's nothing to worry about, she should expect this.

"Captain, I checked. It isn't the Empire's number. Do you remember Nelutho? That bounty hunter. The nekrozzro."

Nelutho... the name sounds familiar. "Kind of. I hate bounty hunters."

Urkaits shakes his head. "Not that one and his small team. He never worked for the Empire."

"Nekrozzro, those with yellow scales and horns."

"Yes, that. A while ago, he kicked a group of traffickers' asses. That one."

Ah, now I remember. Can't say he and I know each other, but I've heard of his name. Not one the Empire's puppets.

I ask, "Is he the one attacking us?"

Urkaits shakes his head. "No way, unless he somehow gained a lot of crew. He has five members, I think. He doesn't like to move in a big group, so that's that. I think it is the Empire chasing behind us. But I'll check the phone, and then we'll know whether it was this woman."

She murmurs. "It's not me. I didn't tell anyone you are here."

I hiss. "But you said you did."

She grimaces. Her chest rises and falls as she seems to be gathering her courage. "I... I... Will you promise not to fly back to the inn?"

There's nothing for me to fly back to, especially when it might be the Empire chasing us. We'll be safer if we go deeper into the Alliance's region.

Not that I fear the Empire; I just don't like to put my crew at risk. We are here to annoy the Empire and slowly chip away at them, not to crash head-on with them all the time.

To her, I say, "Yes."

"Do I have your word?"

I growl. "I'm the leader of my fleet. What else do you want?"

She squirms and inches back, backing onto the stairs that will lead to my seat. "I... I only said that so you wouldn't hurt the two of them. They're like family to me."

Ah... No wonder the horrid look on those two's faces. They knew she didn't call the Empire and lied. They also knew the consequence of admitting that. I could have killed her on the spot.

If that really is the case, maybe I'd have some respect for her. It's not easy to risk her own life for two other beings that are like family, but not family.

What does that mean, though? If she has nothing to do with the attack against us? Should I go and put her back in her inn?

I glance at the window. Near the corner, there's a map of where we are heading. We are getting close to a portal now, something that will get us further away from the Empire and the Alliance. If it is the Empire attacking, when they know that their attack has failed, there's no telling whether they will try again, or be there waiting for us.

She cowers to the side, staring at me with those eyes that are swimming with tears.

I don't know what to do with her...

Rarely does that happen. But also rarely do beings dare to lie about something like that.

Urkaits says, "I didn't find anything. I tried to recover deleted stuff and went through that. Nothing."

I take the phone from him and glance at it myself. There's no calls and no messages that have a hint of connection to the Empire or their many shadow organizations.

So... either she is an expert spy, or she really had nothing to do with the attack.

My cock twitches. But she's here now. I'm not going to let her go.

She lied to me. She's mine now, for what she had done.

I take a shaky breath. Does that count as taking innocent Alliance beings hostage?

She's still watching me, shaking.

I clear my throat. She lied, and I would have killed a few more enemies if she and her two employees hadn't interrupted and wasted my time, so she's not innocent at all.

She asks, "So... you know that I didn't call the Empire now."

"Have you ever worked for them?"

She shakes her head. "No! I've never worked for them. I run the inn and that's it."

And from how empty that place is, she isn't very successful at that. Or say, that isn't a good location for an inn unless she plans to serve beings like me. But since she doesn't have pleasure workers there, I don't know how that will work.

The broadcast says, "We are two minutes away from the portal, please get ready."

I grab her and lift her from the floor. "Your days with your inn are over now. You know what you have done."

"What?" She yelps as I pull her down the corridor to my room. "I thought you figured out I didn't call the Empire!"

"You still lied to me. You will be punished for that."

Chapter 7

Tlezus

I toss my cute little woman onto my bed. She stares at me. Doesn't seem to be as scared as she was before we entered my room. Maybe she's smart and knows what I'm going to do.

The ship shudders as it dives into the portal. I'm fine standing and taking the shakiness, but I'm not sure about her. She'll be safer on the bed. My bed.

She squirms and inches back as I head toward her. "Please, Tlezus. I never wanted to hurt your crew, and I never did."

I snort. "I could have destroyed my enemies even more if your two employees didn't waste my time."

"They are good beings. They didn't call for the Empire either. They worried about me."

Oh, that I know, but it doesn't mean I'm not punishing her. "Kneel on the bed with your ass in the air. Bad females will be spanked."

She grimaces but does as I say. At least she knows enough not to argue with me. There are a lot of things I can do to her, but I'm not sure whether she will like those.

My cock twitches. A lot of things.

"Are you ready?" My tail taps her ass. She's still in her jeans; that's wrong. "Hmm... strip."

She takes an abrupt breath. "You want to see me naked?"

"Do it already. Or do you need me to do that?"

Her mouth opens and closes when she is trying to gauge whether I'm angry at her or playing with her. Interesting.

She reaches to the edge of her t-shirt, pulling it off her, revealing that soft, and pale skin. So different from us, so tempting to devour.

I grit my teeth; my eyes are glued to her movement. There's no way she can't take off her clothes quicker. She's going so slow that it burns me. Maybe she thinks that she has some power over me. I'll prove her wrong. She'll have a taste of her own medicine and regret this.

Her boobs jump out of her bra when she removes that. Her hair drapes over her shoulder, so tempting to pull on.

She asks, "Is this good?"

What? She's only half-naked, not good. But is that a reference to how she's trying to be a tease?

"Strip, completely, now."

She undoes the button and the zipper on her jeans, revealing her pink undies. I saw them last night when I used her like a slut, but dammit... she makes me hard.

Her eyes are on my cock, watching for my reaction. Even here, at my mercy, she still wants to flirt and play with me as if we were still in the inn. Brave, but she'll pay the price of that soon.

Wait... is that a soaked mark on those undies? Is that... hmm... did she get wet when I touched her during the search? This woman is more than I expected.

She tosses her jeans to the side, her tasty long legs inviting a nibble or two.

I say with as flat a voice as I can manage. "Those, too."

She pulls on the edge of her undies, showing just enough of that line between her legs. "Just like that? I'm stripping myself?"

I try my best to keep my tail still. This woman is insufferable. She must think she has seen through me. "Are you going to do that before I do it? It may hurt."

She pulls off her undies. "Kneel on the bed? Ass in the air?"

"Yes, do that now."

She does, with her legs spread and her pussy already glistening with her juice. I smirk when she can't see my face anymore. She's up for some fun. Some torture that will serve a horny bad female like her well.

I get closer, tapping my tail on her ass. It's soft and looks like she will mark up perfectly.

"Argh!" she yelps when my tail lashes her. Her body whimpers.

"Count."

"One..."

"Ouch! Two..."

My heart swells and hammers quicker with every lash. There is red on her ass. So beautiful. I rest a hand on her lower back. "Stay still, or I'll make you start over."

She murmurs. Her pussy is even wetter now, having too much pleasure from this. I lift my hand, spanking her. Her ass jiggles and she almost falls. Beige skin is so pretty.

I blow cool air on her ass. She shivers. Her pussy is dripping with juice now. "Looks like you're enjoying this, slut."

She moans when I shove a finger into that soaked hole. "Tlezus, I'm sorry. I shouldn't lie."

I move my finger in and out of her pussy. Her wall squeezes against me, refusing to let me pull from her. Such a good pussy, so good at taking me.

She's such a natural. I know some pleasure workers try their best to act like that, to be business-ready. But Astrid... she isn't one of those, and she isn't even trying to act that way.

I nibble on the very smooth and fine skin. She yelps but stays in her position. She's so perfect. I'm not letting anyone else have her. She's mine. Mine to fuck with and mine to punish. They call me a bandit. Maybe it's time to do some bandit things.

"Tlezus... don't eat me."

"Oh, I'll eat you up."

She gasps. Maybe she regrets that now. I blow air at her pussy; she is contracting hard, dripping that shiny juice. I reach out with my tongue and slurp her juice. She tastes great.

"Mm... Tlezus..."

I grab her ass, burying my tongue into her hole. It seems I can't lick her dry. I flick her little bud, and she moans so hard.

Maybe that's really the thing giving her all the pleasure, just like how I played with it last time.

I suck that bud, teasing it with my teeth. She squirms and her body arcs to let me lick her deeper. I've never tasted a woman before. This feels so right.

Dammit, my cock is so hard that it hurts. "You are such a slut, loving every moment of this?"

She moans as if that's her answer and her tease. She thinks there's no way I can punish her?

I climb onto the bed, shoving my cock into her pussy. Her wall wraps around me, pulling me deeper into her while she screams.

Is she in pain? I don't like that. Or... is that excitement?

From how her pussy sucks my cock, she's definitely more turned on than in pain.

"Yes!" Her legs move, even though she is still kneeling well.

I spank her ass as I drive myself deeper into her. She's so tight. It's hard to imagine how this small body can take my cock so well, but this is so good that I can't stop myself.

"Harder! Fuck me! Yes!" Now she has completely forgotten that I'm here to punish her. How rude.

I shove my tail into her mouth. "Shut up, slut. Lick me."

Her moans are stifled, but her tongue... She licks the bands of my tail, which is the second most sensitive spot of a baekex, just a tiny bit less than my cock. The tip of my tail can feel the weakest vibrations, and when she licks and sucks my tip as if her life depends on it...

I pound her pussy, my cock swelling even more, stretching her tight hole for myself. I'm going to take every bit of her and make this pussy mine.

I growl when she grabs my tail, taking it into her throat. She said she has never met a baekex before, but she knows how to please a baekex tail. Even better than some attempts of those who are supposed to be experienced pleasure workers.

This is so good, so tempting for me to come inside her. I wanted to last time, but now, it's even more tempting to do just that. She will look amazing dripping my cum.

I silently growl at myself. This isn't about that, not right now. I have something else planned for her.

Her pussy is clenching even tighter around me, squeezing harder and harder with my every stroke.

I pull my tail out of her mouth and miss the warmth at once.

Anyway... "Is my little slut ready to come?"

"Yes! Tlezus!"

Chapter 8

Astrid

My pussy squeezes Tlezus's huge cock. He's so good, so amazing. I love how he pounds my pussy and makes me his.

I'm so close to an orgasm, I can almost feel it. He drives a few long, hard thrusts into me and—

"No!" I scream when an emptiness chews at me.

Tlezus pulls out of me right before he will shove me over the line. How can he...

He lets go of my ass and I drop onto the bed. My pussy contracting and the flame inside my stomach chews at me.

"Tlezus..." Maybe it's dumb, but tears start dripping down my cheek. I need him, I need to come on his cock.

His tail dangles in my face. I snatch at him, but right before I can touch him, he moves away.

He snickers. "Look at you. I told you this is a punishment for how you lied to me and how you wasted my time."

Fuck... When he drove his cock into me, ramming into the deepest part of me, I'd forgotten that completely.

"I'm sorry! Tlezus! Please forgive me!"

He grabs me and rolls me over to face him since I don't have an ounce of strength in me to even move my own body. He's a bit too amazing. I can't resist him. Not even close.

Now, he's staring at my empty pussy with a hungry gaze. His large purple cock, shiny with my juice, is right there in front of my entrance. He can give me all the pleasure I can want, but at the same time... He won't give me any.

"I'm sorry."

"You're going to be my little slut."

"Yes! I will do everything."

"Hmm..." He tilts his head to the side, watching me as I squirm around. I'm facing him, so I can't even rub my pussy on the sheets. And his body parts my legs, so I can't rub my thighs together either.

"Please, Tlezus! I'm all yours. Fuck me, take me hard!" I need the high. The emptiness is so hard to bear. It will kill me.

He smirks as he enters me again. His hot cock fills me well, so good that it drives tears from me.

This must be dumb. Why would I even beg and cry for his cock? This must be him. He ruined me with his cock.

I shiver when what he said last night resurfaces. He said I would beg for him and touch myself thinking of his cock. I laughed at that when I first heard him, but... now... maybe he has a point, and...

"Tlezus! More!" I kick and arch, moving to take him in and out of me when he is inside me but not moving, not doing a thing. This is worse than when he stared at me with that tasty rod out of my body. "I will never lie to you again. Please!"

"Such a slut. Will do anything to get a good cock."

"Please forgive me." I need him. He knows that.

Maybe all the spanking and all the teasing were to set me up like this, to be fucked and teased.

Maybe this is what he will do when I try to tease him with the stripping. He is shoving the punishment into me now.

He moves, slowly, teasingly. "You really should learn a lesson. Should have learned long ago. You are mine now. You don't get to make the call. I'm the one in control."

"Yes, you are the captain, Tlezus!"

He slowly picks up speed. His thick and rough cock stirs my insides, lighting a fire that burns me alive. I clench onto the bedsheet, spreading my legs wider to take his cock.

It doesn't take long before he gets me to the edge again. His cock is so perfect!

I moan and squirm. I'm so close. My pussy squeezes him hard, taking in every rub. I'm dangling on the line, but he is moving just enough to keep me there. My orgasm is so close, yet so far away.

"Tlezus!"

He smirks. "Are you going to be a good female now?"

"Yes, I will be good."

"Be my slut?"

"Yes, that."

"Take my cock wherever and whenever I want?"

"Yes! Use my holes. Fuck me with your cock. Fuck me with your tail."

"Good. And you're mine now."

"Yes, make me your fucktoy!"

I never imagined I would ever say something like that. Shame and guilt burn inside me. How can I let a bandit fuck me and make me a mess like this?

Maybe I should have seen this coming when I lied to him and when he decided to put me on his ship.

But... that's not because I wanted his cock. It was so that he would spare Keeyna and Luekotz. I'm not doing this for selfish reasons, not at all.

So maybe he fucked me so amazingly well and made me come more times than I could count and remember last night, I didn't trick him into kidnapping me to his ship and his bed... Definitely not what I wanted.

Tlezus grabs my boobs, pinching my nipples as he pounds my pussy again.

"Come for me, come on my cock. Scream my name."

"Tlezus! Yes! Fuck me! I love your amazing cock!"

He rams deep into me. An orgasm explodes inside me.

My body shakes from the high, my head throws back, and my toes curl.

He's still in me, taking my pussy hard and fast, every thrust chipping away at my senses.

I can't think. His cock and how good he is are the only things left in my mind. He can make me his fucktoy all he wants.

No, I will beg to be that, beg for him to make me that.

He grunts. "Such a good slut. Born to take my cock. This time, I'm going to fill your womb with my cum, and you will know who owns you."

"Tlezus! You own me! Yes!" My voice cracks when his hot cum shoots into the deepest part of me.

His cock grows larger as if it is blocking his cum from dripping out of me. He fills me completely, but with his cock in me like that, my belly expands, getting filled more and more with his cum.

"Astrid..." His voice is a low growl, shaking deep into me. Just that voice makes me come again.

My pussy milks his cock, ignoring how full I already am. I need him. I need every drop of him.

He pulls out of me, and his cum drips out of me. My stomach is so full of his cum.

"Your pussy..." He grunts and looks at me. He must be happy with how... he made me beg for him. And... he made me crave him...

Just like he warned me...

Chapter 9

Tlezus

My cock twitches as I watch Astrid in a messy pile on my bed. Some of my cum drips out of her, but she holds most of it well. Her pussy is still contracting, but not much is oozing out of her now.

"So good at taking cum. Tell me, are you such a slut to every male that walks into your inn?"

She shakes her head. Her cheek is a tasty pink, almost red.

I pinch her clit and she moans. "I thought you promised to never lie to me again."

"I... I didn't lie. I'm not that. Not at all. I mean... I've had sex before. But not like that. I've never just gone and touched my male patron's cock and let them take me to their beds."

"Really?" My heart skips a beat. How will I know whether she is saying that to please me or whether that's the truth? It sure makes me feel special.

But at the same time, maybe she knew about me when I arrived. Usually, inns don't like to serve beings like us, for obvious reasons. But maybe she didn't dare to refuse us when we outnumbered them by a lot and there was no way she could beat me.

She decided that she should serve me. And when I asked for pleasure workers, she decided that she would be the one to please me.

I'm not sure how I like that thought when she started out fearing me. I've never threatened females into having sex with me, and I hate that idea. But with how she moaned and screamed, I couldn't be forcing her to do that. Besides, she touched my cock first, so she can't blame me.

Inside the room, there is only her panting voice. My cock twitches as she struggles to even move an inch. That's how hard I've taken her. Nice.

"Tlezus..."

"Yes?"

"I... are we good now?"

I take a breath. I would love to tell her that I'm still going to punish her, and I'm going to do that again and again, but that... doesn't sound like me. I'm not that kind of male. "Yes. And we shall be good as long as you remember what you promised me."

"Yes, I remember."

I watch her for another moment... I should go back to the command center and look for a good place for the night for my crew. They know I've taken Astrid. I share my loot with my crew, so I have to let them get some pleasure from the hard work.

Within a short time, we kicked the Empire in the balls more than once. My crew deserves something amazing.

But... looking at Astrid squirming and whimpering on the bed isn't helping. I'm still hard, and I still want some more of her tight and soaking-wet pussy.

I look away from her naked body and her pussy that still has my cum on it. "You take a rest here. Be smart and don't try to act like you can flee from here. You can't. And if you dare to get out of here without my permission, you know what will happen."

She shivers. I made her cry with the edging. I'm good at making her come and giving her pleasure. I can also starve her with that.

"Astrid, I can't hear you."

She gasps. "I know. I will stay here and wait for you."

I nod. "Good. If I don't see you here, on my bed, when I get back, you'll regret it."

I dress, putting on my trousers again. It sucks to have to shove my hard cock back there. I could keep going, but she would break. I have all the time in the world to devour her. Patience is a virtue... probably.

I get out of the room after I clean my tail. There's no need to let others know the things I've done to her. They probably suspect, but they don't need a reminder of that.

The corridor is quiet. The ones that aren't on shift are probably taking a break. I head down the path while my boots hit the ground, the clicking of the heels echoing through the place.

Urkaits is turning the same corner. I almost bump into him.

He bows his head. "Captain, I was about to look for you."

"What's that about?"

"I'm thinking about our next destination. How about we stop at Vammos?"

"A space station?" Usually, a planet is safer to land on. Space stations are filled to the brim with eyes.

"Well, it is Vammos, though. I don't think they care. Not to mention, they will love the business we can bring them. We may be able to sell off our loot there. That will be challenging to do on the planets we used to land on."

"I will think about it." I continue down the corridor to the command center as Urkaits follows me. I don't know how I feel about space stations. Is it safe? Or will we be walking into danger that will be hard to get out of?

There, we will be watched by the owner of Vammos. I've heard rumors about that male. Other than rumors, there are more details about what happened recently.

Nelutho stopped the auction of kidnapped beings there. From what I've heard, the owner of Vammos had to choke up all the money he got from those traffickers because of the security issue, and he's desperate for money to refill his bank.

I don't like kidnapping beings, let alone selling them. But the owner of Vammos will turn a blind eye when he stands to earn something.

If that's the case, Vammos will be happy to have us. The problem is, will someone from the Empire also be there?

Vammos is famous for shady deals. It's within the Alliance's region, but they aren't that eager to crack down on a place that will happily sponsor a lot of the effort in guarding the planets against the Empire.

We arrive at the command center. My crew stands to greet me while I wave for them to focus on work instead.

We are still in the portal. Vammos is on the other side of the Alliance's region. That will make sure we are far away from the Empire's threat.

I ask, "Have you checked with the Fleet? How're the other ships doing?"

"Nothing special to report about. We are all constantly poking at the Empire. Their traders are debating whether they should still wear the Empire's emblem. But as we know, that's an inkling that has been around for a long time now."

I nod. Indeed, the Empire loves whatever way it can exert its control on every other being, be it with charges and tariffs, or with requiring ships to have their logo. The practice won't stop. Such a group of power-hungry bastards.

I go to my seat and take a sip of water. While allowed for enjoyment when we land on planets and space stations, no alcohol is allowed on the ship so that everyone pays attention to work and what needs to be done to sustain the ship.

"Has any of us gone to Vammos recently?"

Urkaits shakes his head as he stands by my side with his arms folded, both of us staring at the screen. "Not that I've heard of. There may have been brief stops for fuel, but other than that, I don't think so."

I tap my fingers on the panel in front of me, checking the map. The portal is taking us all the way over to Vammos. It's close to the exit. No wonder Urkaits suggested that. "A bit too easy to track if the Empire is on our tail."

"But we will know that easily. This is the only portal that is opening today. If the Empire decides to chase us, they can only go via this, and we will know whether they are following."

"That's only the case if the Empire doesn't have any pawns in the Alliance's area already. How many portals are there today?"

"Quite a lot. They're going to different places though, not many are heading nearby Vammos. I doubt the Empire will attack Vammos. That's a place they also get some of their money. They won't kill their golden goose just because of us."

"I'll ask Olith about that."

"Sure, that's a good idea."

I stand from my seat and go to look for Olith and Urkaits follows me. Maybe he's in his reading room. He's usually there unless there's something important happening.

The two guards on the way bow their heads as I walk past them. Maybe I should get a guard in front of my room to keep Astrid inside instead. But she should know what to do. Her phone is with me. There's no way for her to reach anyone else.

"Captain."

"Yes?"

"The woman..."

"What's about her? You've found out more?"

"I'm just curious. You've never kept a female on the ship before."

"Yes." I don't know what he's going for. I'm the rules. Of course I can have a female on my ship and have her on my bed.

Urkaits takes a moment; maybe he isn't sure whether I will be mad at him for what he is going to say.

I ask, "Does that affect how you and the others respect me?"

His tail flinches, but he shakes his head. "No, we know that you are our leader and you will slay the Empire."

Such formulaic words that have little meaning. Sounds like he's only saying that because he feels that he should.

I clear my throat. "I see no reason for you to hide things from me."

"I... I'm just curious. I know you didn't bring her to the ship to get her in your bed, Captain. But... if we are keeping her prisoner, she shall be locked up in the cells. I looked into her and the inn more. She looks like nothing special, just a resident of Edezon. It looks like her family has been living there for generations now."

"So? If I want to keep her in my room, what's the problem?"

"Or... it's Vammos. Maybe we can get extra money—"

I spin around and glare at him. He stumbles to a halt. I snarl. "Urkaits, what are you hinting at? We are warriors, we aren't traffickers. There is no honor in selling beings."

"Well, she tricked us. I think that puts her separated from other beings. We can sell her as part of our loot."

"No." I resist the urge to punch him in the face. I don't sell beings; the Fleet has never and will never do that. "Urkaits, I'm not joking with you. We don't do that. Do you need me to repeat that?"

He bows his head. "I'm sorry, Captain. Maybe my question should be, what are we going to do with her?"

Keep her in my bed and let her please my cock.

"We will figure that out later."

We arrive at Olith's door, which is good because I have no interest in continuing that conversation. I'm not handing Astrid over to anyone, and I'm absolutely not selling her to beings that will probably torture her. If she's going to be someone's plaything, she's going to be mine.

I knock, and Olith calls us to come inside. He's sitting on a couch with his legs crossed, reading on his tablet.

I give him a nod. "How are you doing?"

"All is well." He puts his tablet on the coffee table. "What's this about?"

I ask, "We are considering going to Vammos and spending the night there. Let the crew have some fun and celebrate. Do you think Vammos is a good location?"

He blinks and muses. He often thinks that the crew is a bit too hung up on wanting pleasure. But when all these males are here living under high stress, something has to be done.

We have the training zone here, but when we can't butcher each other and spill blood, that isn't an efficient way for the crew to blow off some steam. Comparatively, getting some pleasure workers is the most non-destructive way.

He says, "I've heard that Vammos is getting braver in who they let in. They have stronger defenses now."

I say, "That won't be enough to guard against the Empire if things happen."

"But will the Empire risk that? Vammos is in the Alliance, after all. If they want to do a full assault, it will be hard to pretend or find a scape goat."

I take a deep breath. "I guess. We aren't the only group of outlaws that specialize in pissing off the Empire. And we probably won't be the only group that's been to Vammos."

Olith nods. "There will always be risks, but I think Vammos won't be riskier than other places."

Actually, when we are here in space, we are the safest. We have an expert level of technology, hiding our spaceships away from both the Empire and the Alliance's patrol ships.

Well, the Alliance doesn't patrol a lot. They don't think that they own the galaxies, not like the Empire.

Urkaits says, "I've heard that they have a good place for the crew to spend the night."

Maybe that's the reason he suggested Vammos. But as long as the risk is under control, no harm in letting the crew make the call, especially when it's about their own pleasure.

Sometimes, the crew talks a bit more with Urkaits. He isn't the leader and they feel safer with him. I'm indifferent to that. Most of those aren't important issues. If they tell me everything, that'll keep me busy for a long time.

I nod. "Then that'll be it. We'll stay in Vammos for the night. Then we'll look for another target from the Empire."

We thank Olith and leave, letting him continue his reading. As soon as the door closes, Urkaits says, "About that woman."

I thought we were done with that topic. He still wants to keep going? I lift my brows at him. He takes a breath, but he says, "Now that we've made sure she isn't the reason we got attacked, we should let her go? Put her on some planet and she can go take care of herself?"

I shake my head. "No, she's staying here. That's the punishment she gets for lying to me."

He's quiet.

I ask, "What? You have any doubts?"

"No, I'm just curious. Usually, we separate pleasure and work."

"I am. She's in the room, not here among us."

"Captain, I mean..."

"Be straightforward with me, I have no interest in waiting. I don't have a lot of patience."

His tail swings in the air. Something is that hard to say out loud? He shrugs. "Just want to be sure. Don't worry, we all know that she's yours."

"Yes." Maybe he thinks that having Astrid here will make me weak. Or he thinks that I shouldn't keep her. If she didn't cause the attack, we captured the wrong human.

It would make the most sense for me to release her. No apology needed when she is the one who lied to me and caused herself trouble. But...

My cock twitches at the memory of how her sweet pussy feels and how good she squeezes me and how she screams my name and how she begs to come on my cock.

There are no rules among baekex ships. No one has ever said that no females are allowed on ships. That never happens, though. For us, if we are certain that we've gotten ourselves a mate, most of us prefer landing and staying on a planet instead of staying out here. Most find the danger not worth it.

But Astrid isn't my mate, she's just here... to be my slut and my cute fucktoy. I'm not letting her go, no way.

I say, "Nothing is going to change. I'm still here to fight against the Empire. We will still be hunting their ships. We shall arrange for tonight first. I know there is restlessness when there are undelivered promises. After that, we will discuss the female."

"Sure, Captain. We trust your decision, as always."

That is what he said, but... I wriggle my tail. Something doesn't seem to be right.

Urkaits is a fellow baekex. He's like a brother to me. There's no reason he would want to hurt me. But... my tail seems to feel something...

Chapter 10

Astrid

So... I'm alone here in Tlezus's room, on his bed, in a mess.

This is a dim room. But maybe this is counted as the lights being on. There are rectangular bands on the walls at the corners of the room that give faint white light.

Ah... not a lot dimmer than the inns when I want to save on utility bills. The lights are always bright enough to indicate that we are open, and when we have patrons, I turn them up.

When Tlezus and his crew arrived at my inn, I didn't turn it up, and they didn't complain. Maybe the dimness is why they wanted to stay there.

The ship is dim, too. When Tlezus first brought me onto the ship, the place he searched me was also dim, and I barely made out who and what was where.

More importantly, now what? What should I do?

Tlezus is out of the room now, leaving me here alone. I... maybe I shouldn't miss his presence.

Ouch... my limbs are all so heavy and tired. My pussy and my ass are sore after he used me hard.

What is he going to do to me? Keep doing this? Fucking me all the time?

I push against the softness of the bed, sitting up instead. His cum is still warm inside me, still reminding me of... all the things he did to me.

My stomach still feels fuller than it usually is; that's pretty crazy.

Where is he? I'm cold.

I put a foot on the floor, then the other, holding onto the bed to stand. My knees are weak and I almost fall back onto the bed. I've never been this exhausted, not from sex.

My clothes are all scattered on the floor. I pick them up and put them on.

This is a strange room. There is this bed I was on, and a tall wooden pillar with hooks that is probably used as his wardrobe. There's a belt there, just like the one Tlezus has, but this one has no weapons. On another hook, there is another robe that looks like it's made of metal; it has a glimmer and buckles that are more like metal. Maybe that thing is heavy and therefore he doesn't wear it.

There is a corridor across the bed, leading somewhere else. I head over there. It won't be a way to flee from the ship, but maybe I can find something useful there.

I walk through the corridor, which leads to a space with a round table in the center and four chairs around it. There are two bean bags by the wall, which face the other side of the wall with a large piece of something on it, maybe it is paper or a piece of cloth. There are drawing and lines on it. It's too dim to see it clearly, but it looks like a map.

I get closer to that side of the wall. It really is a map. It's not about planets though. There are words in a language I don't understand. Tlezus talk in a common language among travelers when I'm the intended listener, but it looks like baekex has their own language.

"Astrid." Tlezus's voice comes from the other side of the room. "Where are you?" That's almost a growl.

I shiver. Am I not supposed to be on this side? Maybe when he told me to wait here for him, he really did mean staying on the bed until he's back, not just staying in the bedroom.

He will find me shortly, so there's no point hiding. "I'm here, this side, near the table."

"I said wait for me on the bed," he growls. He's coming here, his footsteps shaking the room.

"I'm sorry!" I take a step back when he shows up at the entrance to this side of the room. There's something in his hands. Looks like plates or some kind of container.

Oh... there is the smell of some herbs and meat, and there is also bread. Is that food?

Maybe food for him?

I hope my punishment is over and it doesn't include sitting there watching him eat while I'm starving. I don't remember the last time I've eaten, maybe some snacks here and there when I flirted with Tlezus yesterday? Gosh, that feels like so long ago. I was planning to eat, but his crew showed up. Then... I didn't get a chance to get something proper into my system.

He heads over to the table and put down the food. "What are you doing here?"

"Um... Curious? I saw the corridor from my bed. I thought I was good as long as I stayed inside the room."

"Come here." He stands by the table with his arms folded. I doubt he's in a good mood...

"Sure... I'm sorry."

I head over to him. Will he beat me up? Or edge me again?

His tail isn't moving much; maybe that means that he's serious and tense. Because I'm not in the bed? He thinks that I'm trying to flee?

He gestures at the chair by his side, so I sit. He sits by me and pulls the food closer to us. "Eat."

Oh... "These are for me?"

There are six pieces of bread, all large since I'm smaller than the average baekex. The large bowl of something that looks like meat curry smells amazing. My stomach is rumbling and I can't wait to eat, but...

"Yes, eat." His tail wraps around my waist, pulling me to him while he takes a piece of bread for himself. "For you, and also for me."

I take a piece of bread like he does. There are no eating utensils here. This room is so dim that I can't see colors well. The bread is light in color, probably. It's cube-shaped, like a small loaf of bread.

He tears his into half, dipping it into the stew. He scoops up a few pieces of meat that look like steak and eats it.

I haven't eaten like this before and I've never tried something like this. Looks interesting. I do the same, tearing a piece of bread. I dip it into the stew; it's thicker than I expected. I shove it into my mouth, but the bread gets soft from the stew and almost drops. I barely catch it with my hand.

He laughs. "You're silly. Should have done that quicker." He uses the last of his piece of bread, scooping up the food. "If you're too slow, it drops."

I do as he did, but the piece of bread is a bit too big for my mouth, and some of the onion fall on the table.

He chuckles again. "You are so cute."

"I thought you are mad that I left the bed and came here?"

He shakes his head. "I'm just wondering where you went. If any of my crew dares to touch you..."

"Ah, I see."

He wraps an arm across my waist, next to his tail that's already on me. "I won't let anyone hurt you."

My heart flutters. "I thought you'll just leave me alone until you wanted to fuck me again."

He strokes my side as he finishes the piece of bread he demonstrated with. "I'm not that." His voice is strangely cold though.

"Is anything wrong?"

"No, nothing you should worry about."

So there is something?

He takes another piece of bread, tearing it into smaller pieces with his teeth. "I'm the leader of the ship, so there will always be something to worry about and something to plan for."

Probably.

He holds me tightly while he eats, stumbling his way when he only has a single free hand.

It's a nice stew with nice herbs that are mixed right to optimal. It isn't spicy, but the juicy taste of it lingers even after I swallow. The meat is tender and well-cooked. There are finely cut pieces of potatoes or some type of starchy plant. My stomach rambles even when I'm eating. I could eat more of that, all day.

Somehow, it feels good to be here, eating with him. I thought he would give me random and disgusting food that is only good enough for me to not die, but he's here eating the same type of food as me.

Maybe he doesn't see me as a prisoner? Or... just slightly better than that?

I take another bite of the bread, learning how to tear a piece that's the right size to scoop up the meat and at the same time fit my mouth.

As I swallow it, licking the sauce that's on the corner of my mouth, the map across catches my eyes again.

I ask, "What's the map of? Where is that? Your home planet?"

"Was. Not exactly my home planet. We consider that the baekexes' home planet, but I've never been there in my lifetime."

"Oh..." Something bad must have happened.

He takes a breath, slowly letting it out. He puts the piece of fresh bread on the table. Maybe what I asked has spoiled his mood for food. "I suppose... I don't have to tell you. But... it's not a secret anyway. My planet's story isn't that unique. The Empire..."

I halt my breath as the tension inside him spikes.

He says, "Baekexes used to live there. My family had a ranch there, had been generations by then. But those from Thrizek came and took everything away from us.

My family fought against them, but failed and were chased out of the planet, barely fleeing quickly enough to not be eliminated. Maybe one day, hopefully within my lifetime, baekexes will go back to our planet."

"So..." I shiver. It... is scary to wake up one day and be robbed of everything. "Your family and baekexes have been living on ships since."

He nods. "Quite a lot of us. Scattered baekexes grouped and formed the Fleet, which has a lot of smaller fleets. We do different things to stay alive. Some are like me. We attack and rob the Empire's ships and their outposts when we can. After they robbed us of everything and kept some of the baekexes that didn't flee quickly enough as their slaves, that's the least we can do. At least for now, until we come up with a way to dismantle it."

The Empire is a large and very advanced civilization. It will be very difficult to stop them. I've learned from history lessons. The Alliance was formed to stop the Empire's expansion, but even then, it took a lot of beings' lives before the Alliance gained its footing against the Empire.

I hug him back. "Sorry to hear that. I don't think there's anything I can say or do to make it better."

"It's okay. Sometimes, I got tired of thinking about that, when, like you said, there's nothing we can do about it. But baekexes won't give up. There are other beings like us too, losing everything because of the Empire."

No wonder he hates the Empire and asked whether I've ever worked for them and whether Nelutho worked for the Empire.

"I've heard of every evil thing the Empire has done to smaller planets."

"Yes, they acted as if they were doing us a favor by taking over our planet. Baekexes had it bad since we are warriors. I used to hate those planets that simply surrendered and I used to think that if we fought as one, we wouldn't have fallen. But the longer I spend out there flying places, the more I realize that it's not that simple. Maybe it's not wrong to stay alive. But sometimes, I'd rather be dead than work for the Empire."

He shudders and sighs. "You are interesting. I've never talked to anyone about this. I suppose my crew all knows about that, so there's no point saying that. Given the nature of my way of living, I don't have others to talk to."

There's a warmth swelling inside me. "Thank you. I feel special."

He gives a few wry chuckles. "Maybe you are."

"And the Empire is the one calling you bandits."

"They do. They hate us just as we hate them. I don't attack ships that don't work for the Empire, if I know that they are that. Sometimes, we misfire and hit the Alliance's ships that are in the Empire's region. I understand trading is trading, but sometimes, I don't know how to feel about that."

He stands and nudges me to follow him. He goes to the map and points at somewhere that should be plains close to the sea. "My father told me that here is where the ranch used to be. He has never been there either. He heard about it from my grandfather, so on and so forth."

Ah... I hold him tighter. Maybe he isn't such a bad being.

Tlezus says, "It's a lot simpler when you run an inn and serve everyone. There are no complex relationships, no history to bear."

"Well... maybe no complex relationships, but history... That's my family's inn, also for generations. We had good days back then, but when tension grew between the Alliance and the Empire, everything changed. Travelers and tourists are pretty much gone. We barely sustain the business. Now... I'm not doing it even as well as my parents. We should relocate, but we don't have the funds to do that."

He hugs me to him, pinning me to the wall to the side, away from the map. His eyes are intense on me. I swallow. His body presses against me as if he wants to fuck me against the wall.

"Astrid... I... Thank you for telling me. And also thank you for listening to my rambling." He cups my cheek. "I don't know whether this is a human thing, or maybe this is about you. I feel better talking to you. I kind of feel that you'll understand."

Oh, Tlezus...

"I try to. I won't completely understand, but I hope I understand well enough."

He smirks. "It's a nice feeling to not be called evil once in a while, not that I don't like being called a bandit. We rob to give to those the Empire hurts."

Maybe it's him, or maybe it's the air. I can't breathe. There's something there between us that sends a shiver down my spine. "That's nice of you. Must be tough when every other being thinks that you're the bad guys."

"It doesn't bother me. Some know what we are trying to do. Those who know don't hate us. I know most groups that are like us. We fund, to our best ability, forces that are our allies and those that stand against the Empire."

I blink. "Maybe this is the reason you landed on Edezon, in the Alliance's region."

"Yes, that's part of the reason. We need to be in a place where there will be beings that don't try to kill us. Part of that didn't work out as intended, but part of that." He runs his finger over my throat. "Works out better than I've imagined."

Is that... He got me? Am I thinking about myself a bit too highly?

There's a beep and there comes a mechanical voice. "Attention, we are landing shortly. Please get ready."

Landing? Landing where? Another planet? Or are they attacking another ship?

Tlezus takes a step back. "Finish your food."

"Mine?" I thought we were supposed to share? He hasn't finished his half.

"I'm not hungry. You can have the rest. Get ready for the landing. You will go with me."

"Where are we?"

He watches me as I walk over to the table. "You will know it when we get there."

Ah... Loves to keep secrets? Enjoying the mysterious vibe?

Chapter 11

Astrid

I look around as I leave the ship. Tlezus is already there waiting for me. I should walk down the stairs and join him there.

There are some murmurs from the baekexes behind me, waiting to get out of the ship.

It's bright here compared to the ship. I've never been here before. There are ivory, if not white, metallic walls here. Across from me are a few spaceships. Is this an indoor parking lot?

Before I get pushed down the stairs, I join Tlezus. The baekexes are heading to a wide hallway.

I take a breath when Tlezus's arm wraps around my waist.

The staircases leading to the ship are folded back now. The shining pad that indicates the condition of the door turns green. The door is safely locked now.

All the baekexes are gone now, leaving only Tlezus and me.

Now that his crew isn't around, he pulls me even closer to him. His warmth wraps around me and... there's a warmth pooling in my stomach. That's so embarrassing. The harder I try to think about something else, the more his body screams for me to touch him and feel him.

I should say something to get out of this situation. "What do you want from me? I don't suppose you'll let me go just like that."

He snickers. "Obviously not, not after you've promised to be mine."

I swallow. His tail moves. If there aren't other beings around us, maybe he would have done something more with me.

He says, "I'm not going to leave you on my ship for you to create chaos. So while my crew enjoys themselves, you are coming with me."

I stare at him. I don't suppose he's going to get a pleasure worker for himself while I'm here with him. Or... does he plan to take me again?

My cheek burns when it feels like his cum is still hot inside me. Dammit... What has he done to me? I'm not that much of a horny woman, but he... It must be his problem.

He nudges for me to start walking, so I follow along. He says before we turn a corner, "You remember how you're mine. If you try to flee or do something silly..."

Now that he says that, it's tempting to try. There are more and more beings on the street now. Maybe this is a space station. I don't know this place. There are plenty of beings out there who won't care about me. Maybe... following Tlezus around isn't that bad. At least, he doesn't seem to be hurting me. Until there is a chance I can flee safely.

"Sure, I will follow you around and be a good woman."

He smiles. "Good."

There's a market in front of us, rows and rows of stalls with all different types of beings shopping and looking around.

Now that we are in a public place, maybe I can get him to buy me something. I'm here now, so I may as well make the best use of this.

There's a stall selling some type of dried fruit. I point at that. "Tle—"

He covers my mouth and hisses at me. I swallow and lick his hand when I shouldn't.

After he makes sure I've stopped talking, he takes his hand off me. I lift an eyebrow at him. What's wrong?

Is there someone around that will attack us? I thought he has chosen a safe place for his crew.

He says, "Don't call me by my name here." There's no smirk on his face, but a tension that lingers in him. He isn't joking at all. Maybe it's like Nelutho has warned me. Tlezus is a bandit, while not everyone knows exactly who he is or look like, maybe more will have heard of his name.

"Okay, Barney."

He lifts my brows at me. I don't know why I thought that, either. Tlezus is the baekex that loves to think that I'm his and he's keeping me locked up for as long as I will allow him to. He's not cute like Barney.

He lifts my chin and forces my eyes to him. "What's Barney?"

"Your name now."

He sneers. His tail flicks as if he is warning me about the whipping and how he edged me and made me beg to come.

I shrug. "He's a dinosaur. Purple, just like you. Have you heard of dinosaurs?" It will be dumb if I have to keep explaining one thing with the other.

He blinks, seemingly giving that some thought. "Lizard? Some are big and some are small. Has four limbs. Some can fly. Existed a long, long time ago. Those?"

I nod. That's not too far away. "Yes, dinos. Barney is a purple dino."

"Okay." He lets go of my chin. "What were you pointing at?"

"Those dried fruits, they look tasty." Before I can think about it, I hold his hand and start walking. His hand is larger than mine and warm like the rest of his body. There's a spark in the air when our hands touch. Am I the only one feeling that?

He lets me pull him over to that stall regardless. "Are you hungry? Still?"

My heart skips a beat. Is he simply asking about the fruit? Or about something else? Say... the thing between his legs?

He has that naughty smirk again. If he wasn't before, he's thinking about that now.

I nod and point at a pack of dates. "Please? Can I try some of these?"

He rolls his eyes, but he picks it up and pays for it. "Whatever you like, yes, you can get it."

Oh… I wasn't expecting that. I thought I was here as a prisoner or just a fucktoy for him. Maybe he will give me food to keep me alive, but buying me extra stuff?

Speaking of which, maybe he could have locked me up on the ship. This is a group of bandits. They ought to have some facilities to lock beings up.

He's watching me now. I open the bag and lift one to his lips. "You want one?"

He eats it from my fingers. His lips touch my fingers. His eyes widen for a split second, but he soon schools himself. His face is a bit too cold now. Does he not like the dates?

I eat one. It's sweet, but not too sweet that I need water after eating one. He's staring at me, that intense gaze… Is he fucking me in his mind? Or at least undressing me? Or… he wants to see through me?

His tail is moving, the tip dancing around, not like how he usually is.

Maybe he feels my gaze on his tail, because it stops moving around.

I lift another date to him. "Do you want one more?"

He shakes his head. "You wanted them. You can have more."

"You don't like it? Not a fan of sweet things?"

Now that I think about it, I don't remember asking him. When we served them snacks in the inn, they were fine with the food. In fact, they ate a lot. But we didn't serve them anything sweet. When he brought in the stew and the bread, there was also nothing sweet.

Do baekexes not like sweet things?

He gently squeezes my arm. "Sweet is fine. I'm not a picky eater. These are pretty rare, so you should have more since you like them."

"Okay." I eat the one that's between my fingers. I lick my finger clean... as clean as it can be. After that, I zip up the bag and put it in my pocket. I love anything sweet. Dates cost quite a bit since the plant is picky. The planets that produce dates are far away from where I live, or for now, lived.

I silently grimace at the thought. Tlezus won't let me go back there. He's a bandit and we live different lifestyles. I want to be back there. Maybe the inn is struggling, but at least that's my home.

Speaking of which, how are Keeyna and Luekotz doing? I hope the landlord won't give them a hard time. Luekotz has been around longer than Keeyna. Maybe he will be able to handle the business, which, sadly, won't be busy for him.

I miss them.

Wait... if it was the Empire's beings that attacked Tlezus... will they go back there to search for traces of his crew? What will they think about the two of them? They, we, are innocent and we don't know a thing about Tlezus's crew other than they are bandits. The Empire won't blame the two of them for their failed attack, right?

He stops when we arrive at a crossroads, and he nudges me to the edge of the market, where there aren't as many beings around. "How are you doing? Are you fine?"

I take a shaky breath, slowly letting it out. "I am fine. I..."

He points at me, his tail behind him threatens and reminds me of what I have promised him.

"Barney... Don't be mad at me."

His gaze softens slightly. He nods. "Tell me what's in the beautiful head of yours."

"I... Is it possible for me to make a call back to the inn? Hey, you promised not to be mad."

I reach for his cheek. He lets me touch him, but the tension inside him is growling.

I say, "I want to make sure the two of them are safe. And... I don't want them to worry about me."

He hisses. "You want to go back there?"

I shouldn't, right? But I also promised not to lie to him. But... he is a bandit, must I take what I promise him seriously? He was threatening me with an orgasm when he made me promise him.

"No, that's a failing business. If I'm kidnapped, maybe I won't have to carry the debt with me anymore. No one will blame me. The two of them don't have a name on the lease, so they can't be blamed either. My disappearance will be for the best."

There is an invisible hand squeezing my throat. I barely keep my voice together, not letting it crack. Maybe everything I said is accurate and is actually the case, it cuts deep into me as I utter the words.

I clench a fist. Tears threaten to spill out of me. I turn away, but he cups my cheek and makes me look at him. "If all you want is make a call, yes, you can do that."

He pulls my phone out of his pocket and hands it to me. "Do it here."

I nod. I turn it on and search for Luekotz's number. Hopefully, they are safe.

I press the button and lift the phone to my ear. It goes through, the ticking sounds hammer into me, sending my blood frozen.

Please take the call?

Please?

Tell me you are alive?

Tell me you are safe?

The call clicks. "Hello."

It's Luekotz!

I open my mouth. It's him, I should greet him, but I can't manage a single word. Now Tlezus is frowning at me. I say, "Luekotz, is that you?"

"Astrid! How are you? Are you safe? Did those purple beings hurt you? Are they listening to your call? Oh... I bet they are."

It's rare for Luekotz to say that much. I worry about him too, so much so my hand is shaking. A pair of arms wrap around me. Is that a warning from Tlezus?

Tlezus kisses my forehead with a weak smile. He holds me close as if he's trying to comfort me or make sure I won't fall. He may be smart since I'm lightheaded and my knees are weak. I've been hearing Luekotz's voice every day for longer than I can remember, but nothing compares to this.

"Luekotz, I'm so happy to hear your voice. I'm safe. They didn't hurt me. They figured out... I wasn't the one who caused the attack. They are fine with that."

Tlezus nods, and he strokes my side.

I continue, "How is Keeyna? Is he fine? Safe?"

"He is. We are fine. Edezon's enforcement come to check on us. They think that the Empire attacked us, well, them. They aren't happy and say that they will let the higher-ups know about this incident. The Empire crossed the border, after all."

"So... you guys are still in the inn?"

"No, we aren't. It's chaos there after the fight. The enforcement arranged somewhere to stay until the inn is repaired. The insurance will be covering everything, including an estimate on lost business, so the two of us will be covered for a long time."

A long time? Maybe the insurance company didn't do a good enough estimate on the "lost" business. But why would any of us go and correct them?

I let out a sigh. Tlezus is the reason I'm standing. I snuggle to him as I continue the call. "That's good. I worry so much about the two of you. Stay safe, okay?"

"Sure. I hope... I mean, you also stay safe. Wish you all the best."

"Same, all the best."

We end the call. Tlezus takes the phone away from me with his tail. He watches me. "What did he say?"

I think he heard the call though. Maybe he's testing to see whether I will lie about it. "He said that they are safe. Edezon's enforcement went to check on the inn."

Tlezus tenses up. "And? What did they find? They interrogated your friends?"

"No, the enforcement thinks that the Empire pretended to be someone else and snuck their way in. Don't think they've found a lot about you."

Fuck... If the enforcement asked, maybe Luekotz would have told them about Tlezus...

"That I don't worry. They are smart. They know of my fleet's existence. So us staying in an inn and getting attacked by the Empire is a very reasonable thing. Don't worry about that."

"Huh? I thought..." I shouldn't mention his crew of bandits here. "You like to lay low."

He has a light frown from when I almost slipped. Beings around us are busy looking at stalls, which are on the other side of the road, none are paying attention to us, and none are even slowing their steps. Hopefully, none are eavesdropping on us.

He looks around before he pecks a kiss on my forehead again. Is this the way he attempts to be dating me so that we won't attract unwanted attention?

"Astrid... Are you fine to keep walking?"

"Sure, but you will have to hold my arm."

He chuckles. "Can do."

Maybe it's strange. Being around him isn't as scary as I thought. When he first captured me and yanked me to the ship, I thought I would die an ugly and painful death.

That didn't happen.

Like Tlezus said, I lied to him. But... he edged me badly, but compared to all the different kinds of potential punishments, that's not too bad.

And now... when he doesn't need to let me out of the ship, he did it anyway.

Our arms are linked as we head down the market. He is looking around, seemingly looking for something.

My heart hammers in my chest; his closeness is doing strange things to me. He's a baekex... I'm a human...

Wait... What am I even thinking about? I should be trying my best to flee and go back to meet up with Luekotz and Keeyna, not here thinking about Tlezus's cock and how good he can make me feel.

He stops again. In front of us is an inn, or a hotel, to be accurate. It's a building within this large indoor place. Maybe this place is a space station. I've been to a few, but none this big.

He says, "The crew is staying here for the night."

In a space station like this, there doesn't seem to be day and night. The lighting here is artificial and in theory, can be switched on all the time.

I ask, "What's the time now?"

He checks his watch. "Nine in the evening. That's the time we run for the ship. Space travel, as you can imagine, makes time a bit challenging."

I nod while I can't tear my eyes away from this hotel. It's huge and new, and it has at least ten floors. I know it can't be, but it looks like it is glistening under the lighting. This place is inside a space station, but it's larger than my inn. Across the road, there are a few beautiful females. Maybe those are pleasure workers waiting for their patrons.

If Tlezus wasn't here with me on his arm, maybe they would come over and see if they could get some business off him.

There's a storm in my stomach. Something... that twists my gut swarms inside me. I don't want that.

"Huh?" He watches me. "Are you tired? You're holding me tighter now."

"Oh, not really."

"Or do you want to go inside? I booked rooms for my crew and there'll be a room for me. We can call this a day if you want to."

I shake my head. I don't want to go inside. This has to be a well-established place with a thriving business that's actually busy.

As we are standing here and staring at it, there are beings going in and out of the building with their luggage. When the door swings open, there are a few glimpses from the inside, where there are queues of beings waiting to check in and get their room.

I know it makes no sense to compare my small inn with this one. But... I don't want to see the inside of this place. Even the outside of it reminds me of how much of a failure I am.

Now, I won't even have a chance to be successful with the inn since... Tlezus is planning to keep me as his. He won't let me go back there and work on the inn.

Chapter 12

Astrid

I stare at the hotel. It screams everything that I'm not. Not successful, not good enough, just a dumb woman who doesn't know how to run a business.

What does that mean by staying here with Tlezus? I won't be able to work on what I have been trying to improve on for my whole life. For what? To go and become Tlezus's fucktoy?

Maybe he isn't that evil a being and maybe he does care about me. But he and I... we can't. We want different things in life. Too different.

Tlezus squeezes my hand. "If you don't want to go inside, we can go down the market. We don't land on a space station a lot, so may as well take your chance. I don't think you've been here a lot of times before."

I nod. My legs move on their own when they know that I'm supposed to be following him and I'm supposed to behave well. There should be beings talking around me, footsteps, and ambient noises from all around me. But... all of those are a blur.

Even my hands are numb, as if they have given up on feeling anything.

It's a miracle that I'm even walking and not a mess on the floor.

There are tears and... a hollow pain in my stomach. Tlezus is pretty much dragging me along with him by now. I'm just a body that is moving around. Maybe for him, I'm the pussy he can fuck whenever he wants.

I don't want that.

But... if I stay with him... like I told Luekotz, that would solve a lot of issues relating to the inn. Tlezus will take care of me. Keenya and Luekotz will be fine. They can take care of themselves. If the inn fails, they could go and get another job.

Tlezus...

He looks around, seemingly unaware of my mood. He's looking to the side when he asks, "Seeing another inn makes you think of things?"

It sounds like he's just asking for the sake of killing the silence between us.

"Kind of. I mean, I have been running an inn for my whole life. So... seeing another one in a space station is quite something."

"I see." His voice is flat and gives away nothing.

I continue, "I mean, won't it be great if I can run a better inn? One that's better than the one back on Edezon? I can take care of travelers. There will be fun stories."

He's quiet, seemingly too focused on looking for something, maybe looking for a shop.

What's the point?

I silently sigh. He's a bandit who annoys the hell out of the Empire. I don't like the Empire either, but... his world is so far away from mine, and I've never actually done anything about that.

Do I want to keep going from place to place with him? I don't know how he feels about me. I would love to think he cares about me, but...

When we turn a corner, we get into the streets with shops on both sides, these aren't stalls anymore. These are actual buildings, like the hotel, except most of them are two-floored buildings, so, a lot smaller.

He says, "You know, there are inns on a lot, if not all, planets."

Huh? Is he saying what I think he did?

He says, "I mean, maybe you aren't that bad at running an inn, you just need a better location. A better chance to have a go at it."

I grit my teeth when more tears swell inside me. Why is he talking about that? That won't happen. All he has planned for me is to stay on his bed and spread my legs when he's around, and that'll be my life.

He seems oblivious, which doesn't feel like him. But I'm not going to remind him of my mood. I don't need that. He's going to ask, and he won't be happy with my answer.

Nothing will change, so why bother?

We turn another corner. He lets out a breath. Maybe he has found the shop. It's an old-fashioned shop. Built with wood. The style is a bit like my inn, but it looks a lot more antique than mine. The inside is dim, but maybe that's because of the glass it uses.

Next to the entrance, there is a wooden standing sign. This shop is buying rare items, and also selling those.

Tlezus squeezes my hand. "Will you wait for me here? I'll go do something inside."

"Sure." What else am I going to say? No? That I'm going to take the chance and flee?

If I had a way to get home, maybe I would. But I have no money, and...

Tlezus doesn't look back, he goes into the shop. I don't think he plans to buy from there. Maybe he has something to sell. Given that he's a bandit, having loot to sell sounds normal enough.

Am I going to wait here for him just like this?

Someone taps my shoulder. I spin around. "Sorry, am I in your way?"

That figure covers my mouth and pulls me into an alley.

I kick and stomp when the figure growls, "Shut up, human. It's Nelutho."

Eh? I flinch for a second and he manages to pull me away from the street.

I blink to see the nekrozzro in front of me, with the woman, Kimberly. "Why are you here?"

Kimberly says, "We have no time to talk. The purple thing will come out soon. His fleet is here, so we have to get you out of here right now."

"Huh? But..."

"We went and checked on the inn after catching wind of what happened. Keenya told me what happened and,"

Nelutho hisses, Kimberly pulls on me, "We hurried to be here. Let's go!'

Wait... I glance at the shop Tlezus went into. If I go with Nelutho, I will go back there to the inn which is pretty much hopeless. But if I stay with Tlezus...

Kimberly frowns. "What? You want to stay here with that baekex? You know who he is and what they do."

But if I leave like this... Will Tlezus chase after me? He knows where I live. Maybe he doesn't want to risk getting caught by the Empire, but he may hate being betrayed enough that he would rather take the risk. If that's the case...

If I stay with him, will I be able to convince him that...

Tlezus mentioned inns on other planets, he wasn't mad when I mentioned that I wanted to be running an inn. Is there a chance...

There's a pulse inside me that pulls me to him. It feels right to be with him, but at the same time...

Kimberly stops pulling on my wrist. "Hey, are you sure you want to stay? I mean, we were commissioned to get you back home. But if you don't want to, we won't force you. At the end of the day, you get to decide how to live."

Nelutho pulls his gun. Is he going to shoot me?

Kimberly waves at him, and he takes a few steps, standing between me and the shop. Maybe Tlezus will be coming out very soon.

I take a deep breath. It's now or never...

Chapter 13

Tlezus

It's always nice when the effort spent on missions pays off. I put the coins from selling the necklace and a few loose items into my pocket.

I thank the shop owner again. He's still eyeing the necklace. He's going to turn a profit on that, but I've earned enough from it, too. With how hard he stares at the necklace, he isn't going to talk to me unless Ibuy something else.

I turn around. This place is pretty decent and always offers a good price for our items. It smells like fine wood, which I like. Most importantly, this place isn't stupidly bright like the outside, which makes it good.

Hm... Out of the window, there's no Astrid standing there. My heart skips a beat and my hands run cold when...

Astrid is at the opening of an alley, she's talking to someone.

I squint at that. Hm... Nelutho. What is he doing there?

How dare he puts his hands on Astrid!

I'm about to dash out of the shop, but I stop myself. If I go out now, they will definitely see me. And... What if Astrid wants to leave?

Nelutho is famous for being a creep. He does what he wants to and he doesn't give a fuck to what others think about him. A bit like me, but he's also nosy enough. Maybe he caught wind of what happened in the inn and decided that he should go and rescue Astrid.

That sounds like something he would do. Given Astrid had his number in her pocket, she must have met him before we arrived at the inn. So...

That means Astrid knew who I was when I was there. She pretended she didn't know? Figured there wasn't anything she could do?

I...

I swallow. It will be strange and dumb to stand here in this shop, doing nothing. But... I can't make myself leave.

I want her to stay with me. She's someone I feel safe and comfortable talking to. I don't even find that among my fellow baekexes. She's a human, but...

She has the perfect body and the equally perfect mind. I want her to be here with me. But... what if she's scared of me? And now, what if she decides to leave with Nelutho?

Nelutho will send her back to the inn. That's what she wanted. She will be happy there.

I take a deep breath. It hurts. But... I spent my life promising to crack the Empire, while she's been trying all she can to run her inn.

If she wants to go back there, maybe she should have a chance to do that. Like Urkaits said, she is innocent; we captured the wrong being. I should let her go.

I sigh and fold my arms while I watch from the inside of the shop, through the window, far away from Astrid. Maybe... I should have asked her instead of assuming she would want to stay here just because I said so.

I've always taken what I want, but with her...

I turn away from the alley and pretend to be staring at the display inside the shop. It is a pretty old model ship, well built, and would be nice to put in a living room or something.

If... at least Astrid... whether she's stuck here with me or not won't affect my name. Nelutho isn't someone boastful who loves to broadcast what he has done. He won't go around telling everyone that he took Astrid from me.

She can leave if she wants to. It will be better for her to go with Nelutho, who is a righteous male, than try to flee and run into beings that want to hurt her.

There's a ding at the door. The shopkeeper lifts his head and looks at the door. I don't want to care about that, but... I look regardless, just in case someone's coming after me.

Astrid is there.

What?

I blink and stare at her. Am I seeing things? She was there at the alley talking to Nelutho, right? Is this someone pretending to be her? Because they know I want her to stay here with me? That being thinks that they can sneak onto my ship if they pretend to be her?

She smiles. "Hey, Barney. You're taking some time in here."

Ah... I still don't understand that purple dino, but the Empire's spy won't know about this nickname. "You're here."

"Yes, I wondered why you're still here. Got tired waiting."

I was waiting for her to be gone, but she's here. She should know that if she is here, there's a high chance I won't let her leave me.

What's on her mind?

I pat my pocket with the coins. "I just completed my task. Nothing to look at out there?"

She looks to the side, avoiding my gaze. She doesn't know that I saw her with Nelutho, right?

She reaches for my hand. "I missed you. If you've done the task, let's get going."

I let her drag me out of the shop, which is also what I want. I want to ask her about that. I have to know.

Outside, Vammos is so bright that the light hurts my eyes. I want to pull out my pair of glasses; I have been wanting to, but I don't need the extra attention. Most beings don't wear brightness-modifying glasses indoors.

I ask, "Where do you want to go? You seem to be in a hurry."

She halts, almost slamming into a glojudo, a large mineral-based being that no one wants to scrape by, not to mention slamming into.

"Oh, I didn't think about that. Do you have places to go?"

In fact, I do. I want to get her alone, without any other beings, so that I can talk to her. The hotel room will be great, but knowing myself, we won't be doing any talking there. I don't want to delay that any more than I have to.

Wait... I know of a place that may work this time of the day. "I know of a place with ice cream, fancy a try?"

"Oh, ice cream." She grins. "Yes! You know what I love."

I don't, but I'm glad she likes ice cream. "Come with me."

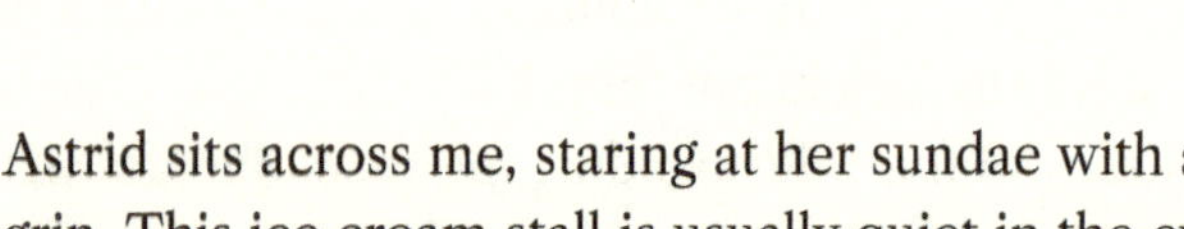

Astrid sits across me, staring at her sundae with a wide grin. This ice cream stall is usually quiet in the evening when most beings have eaten or don't find this place suitable for dinner.

I lick my ice cream cone. She's still staring with a spoon in her hand. I ask, "You said you liked ice cream and you picked this. What are you waiting for?"

She snaps her head at me. "I... Are you sure you don't want some?"

I shake my head. "If I wanted that, I'd order. You can have it."

"Like, have the whole thing? To myself?"

"Yes, you can have the whole sundae, including the blueberry on top."

She stares at me for another moment before she moves her spoon to it. "I've never had something this beautiful before."

Honestly, neither have I. Most of the time, we are on the spaceship, busy making sure we have enough to feed everyone before we reach another destination and can refill, so having nice stuff is lower on the list.

"Good that you love it."

She takes a scoop of the pink ice cream and eats it with a smile. The smile warms me, so much so it might melt me. I won't mind having ice cream with her all the time, everyday, if it pleases her.

I grit my teeth. Maybe I should bring it up, otherwise, it looks like she's going to pretend that she never talked to Nelutho.

"Astrid."

She blinks, swallows her ice cream, and nods. "Yes."

"I have something to ask you." My heart hammers so hard in my chest that it feels like it can jump out of me at any time. This has never happened before. Not even on my first attack against the Empire's outpost.

What's wrong with me?

There's an urge pulsing inside me, making it hard to even sit still.

Maybe I really should ask right now, instead of delaying it till who knows when. She's looking at me, waiting for what I have to say.

"Astrid, I want to ask... Do you plan to stay here with me?"

She gulps. "I... I thought you were going to keep me here, for how I lied to you."

Yes, I said that, but it was for myself, an excuse that I may convince myself and my crew. "I want to know what's on your mind. Do you want to stay here?" And... be my mate?

She shrugs. Before she starts talking, I hiss at her. "You've promised to never lie to me."

"I'm not lying. You thought of keeping me here."

Is she... scared of me?

I say, "I know you met Nelutho just now."

Horror flashes through her face. "I... what are you talking about?"

"I saw him. You were talking to him in the alley right after I went into the shop. He was waiting and I think he wants to bring you home."

She almost drops her spoon. She puts it on the sundae. Her hand is shaking. "Yes, he was there, and he offered to bring me home."

"But you didn't leave with him. Why? You think that I will take revenge on you?"

She shakes her head. I scowl at her. If only there is a way to know whether she's being honest with me...

She says, "No. Or rather, I have thought about that. But... I think I want to stay here with you. I know you won't let me go home and you have other plans for me. But if you want, I want to stay with you."

Does this mean... I know she and I are different and want different things. And... I take a breath; I'm the male, I should ask.

"Astrid, we do have different plans, but I don't hope to make you give up on everything just to cater to me. More importantly, what do you mean by staying with me? I mean, I think I should ask. Do you want to be my mate?"

She watches me with those clear eyes. I grit my teeth. Maybe I should have ordered something that I could put on the table instead of a pointed ice cream cone.

I have never asked anyone that before and I have never even seen getting a mate as part of my life. But Astrid... she's different from every other female that I have met before. I would hate myself and I would regret it if I didn't ask, there's no better time to ask than now.

Astrid

I didn't expect Tlezus to ask that. I thought I was the silly one for thinking that there was a chance he would want me as his mate.

Up until now, it felt like he has more interest in fucking me than anything else. But... maybe our brief talk about the map changed my view of him.

Nelutho was surprised at my decision. I told him that I would stay with Tlezus, and maybe he really is the cute Barney for me. Everything feels right when he's around. It feels right when I'm in his bed and it feels right when we talk about something else, about our goals, about what the ship means for him and the inn for me.

He isn't a human like me, but he and I... are just beings trying to make it in this wide universe, among all the planets. We can feel for each other, something more than sex with each other.

I take a deep breath. "Barney, I'm serious about it. Yes, I will be your mate. I will stay with you. It's different from what I've wanted for myself, but... maybe we will figure out a way."

I have no idea how that will work out, though. But he's my Barney, so it will all work out.

He stares at me as if he has never imagined that. "Really? Astrid..." He holds the ice cream cone with his tail and holds my hands with his. "Yes, I want you to be my mate. I didn't think of asking because I didn't think you would agree to it. When Nelutho was there, I saw it. But I figured if you wanted to leave, I shouldn't stop you. You should be able to enjoy your life. But you're still here."

Indeed, maybe any sane being would have followed Nelutho, since he has the means to send me back home and he would gladly do that.

"Maybe I love you a bit too much, Barney."

He chuckles. "Maybe I will grow to like this name."

Maybe he's no longer that scary compared to when he brought me to his ship.

He reaches for my cheek, and I lean closer to him. Our lips meet, and his are burning hot. His soft lips send fire through me. An electrical spark runs down my spine. There's a pulse of heat inside me. This feels right, like it is how it's meant to be.

His tongue tickles me. I part my lips for him. His tongue stirs all the feelings inside me, maybe I will need more than ice cream to cool myself.

If there was no table between us and no beings around us, we would have done something more.

Maybe part of me knew that when I lied to him. My body knew he would take me to his ship, and he would take me with his cock, but other than that, he would also take my heart with him.

I let out a soft moan, trying my best to tame it down even though we might still be super obvious in a small cafe like this.

He lets go of me, his eyes are dark and he's probably already hard enough to take me. "Maybe I should have taken you back to the hotel, not here."

I know he's a horny male, like what he once said about me — a horny being without horns.

"You have no patience. I love the ice cream, though. It's so amazing to be able to eat the whole sundae on my own."

He shudders and grimaces. I lift my brows at him. Did I say something wrong?

His tail moves and he takes his ice cream cone from it. "Ouch, the ice cream is so cold."

He takes a tissue from the table and wipes his tail. "I should have remembered that I can't put ice cream to the side for too long."

I chuckle. "Looks like I'm not the only one that can't eat properly, so much for laughing at me earlier."

He snorts, but the curl in the corner of his lips has outed him. "Just finish your sundae and we will head back."

"And?" I wink at him. There are no beings nearby, but I still lower my voice. "Next time, I can lick your tail clean."

He swore under his breath. Now I will definitely get what I've asked for, or *worse*, get punished for what I have done.

Chapter 14

Astrid

We head to the hotel straight after I swallow the last mouthful of the sundae.

We go past the lobby and the hallways so quickly that I don't remember how the lobby of the hotel looks and I have no time to wallow in how this hotel is so much more successful than my own inn.

Tlezus, my Barney, takes me all the way to his room, swiping the key card on the door with his tail so that he can push open the door while holding my hand at the same time. It's quite something to watch how a leader of a bandit fleet can be so impatient.

As soon as the door opens, he sweeps me off my feet and takes me to the bed. I smack his chest. "Come on, I can walk there myself."

"Not fast enough."

Maybe he has longer legs than me, but the bed isn't that far away, so the time difference should be negligible. He simply has no patience, or maybe the walk back here has used up all of it, and when there's no one around, he can't hold it anymore.

He puts me on his bed, climbing to join me. This is a large bed that's fit for two big beings like him. My small body alone on this big of a bed would be pretty funny.

Tlezus is naked before I can blink. I have no idea how he did it that quickly. And within seconds, I'm also naked.

He smirks while I'm still staring at him. He's kneeling on the bed, upright. His cock is right in front of me. "What? Like what you see?"

He spreads his arms to the side while he flexes, making those strong muscles even larger and, dammit, he's such a tease. His cock is already fully ready for me, like a nice eggplant, except larger and harder.

I reach for his cock, stroking him. He's so hot, so rough, and will fuck me well. "You want me as your mate so that you can fuck me all the time."

He shrugs. "Well, I've never only considered that. How about you? From how you moaned and screamed every time, maybe all you want is my cock, not me."

"Oh, Barney, how can you say that? I don't only want your cock. I also want your tail."

He growls. There is fire in his eyes. "Seriously?"

"Well, you asked. You know I'm going to be honest with you."

"You are insufferable." He hisses and grabs my hair.

Before he can shove his cock into my mouth, I suck on his huge tip.

Fuck, he's a lot larger in my mouth than he looks and feels in my hands. I lick his tip while my heart pounds in my chest. Maybe he won't break my pussy with this rod, but he can sure choke me with this.

I lick him some more, making my way along his shaft.

He moans and his cock twitches. "Dammit... Shutting you up has never felt this great."

I would have said something if his cock isn't in my mouth. Guess his strategy is working.

"You... stop being a tease!" His cock twitches in my mouth, but he's still not patient even though I'm already working on him. He'll never have enough.

I hold his balls in my hands. He groans. "If you have to keep doing that..."

He holds my hair tighter and pushes himself deeper into my mouth, but a lot slower than I expected. Maybe he knows how large he is and he won't risk killing me.

I try to swallow as much of him as possible, but when his tip hits my throat and goes deeper, there's still a large part of him outside of me.

I stroke his length while sucking what's in my throat. I've never taken such a monster in my mouth before. His size scares me, but I want to do this, especially with that handsome face and how his abs are more apparent when he's sucking in air.

Heat pools in my stomach, threatening to burn me alive. It will feel so good when his cock is buried into my pussy and when he rams into the deepest part of me. My pussy is contracting and I am getting wet. Now, it's complaining about the emptiness.

Tlezus lets out a soft moan. As soon as one of my hands leaves his cock, he growls.

"Mmm..." I choke on his cock as his tail stabs at my pussy and rubs my clit. I part my legs and the tip of his tail rubs me even harder.

I squirm and move some; his tail teases my entrance, getting into me just enough for me to feel him, then pulling from me. I need him...

"Look at me while you suck my cock."

I lock eyes with him while he drives his cock deeper and deeper into my throat. I can't stop myself from swallowing, from squeezing his cock.

He takes an abrupt breath. "You won't get my cum that easily."

Because he wants to fill my pussy instead?

He slaps my pussy with his tail. I moan, and he takes the chance to drill even deeper into my throat. My tongue can almost reach his balls, but not really. But he's definitely choking me by now.

He groans and pulls away from me. "We'll work on that until you can also lick my balls."

I gasp and pant, busy catching my breath when he pins me down on the bed. His cock is even stronger now, barely getting started.

He slaps my pussy with his heavy cock. "What? Are you out already? Can't breathe?"

I roll my eyes. "Not that easily. Or are you the one wanting to bail? I won't laugh at you."

He pinches my clit. I tense and almost got shoved through the edge. He has made me a lot more sensitive than I used to be. It feels wrong, but at the same time, feels so right.

"Astrid, use your beautiful brain before you talk. You know what I can do to you."

"Barney, I also know how much you want me." I arch and rub my pussy against his cock, making him shiny with my juice. "Who are we fooling?"

He growls and thrust his cock into me, stretching me for himself. "Fuck... No matter how many times I've fucked you, you're still so tight."

"Do you prefer it another way?" I moan as the roughness of his rod rubs against my folds. "Oh, Tlezus! Yes!"

He slams against me, hitting me deeper and deeper with every thrust.

I wrap my arms around him, taking every stroke. I move to take him deeper, to enjoy every inch of him.

He squeezes my boobs, pinching my nipples as he devours me.

I'm just the helpless woman here taking a monstrous cock from a large, purple baekex.

"Your pussy is so amazing, so perfect at taking my cock."

"Oof! Give a warning!" I scream when orgasm hits, and at the same time, when his tail assaults my ass, in a good way.

He grunts. Maybe it isn't that easy to penetrate my ass when my back is still on the bed.

He grabs my legs, putting them to the sides of my face, almost folding me in half and baring my holes to him.

"Now, this is better."

"You horny bad baekex."

"Shut up and take my cock." He thrusts into me, pounding me within seconds. He's so deep into me that he may break me. He moves a bit too much that even though his whole length won't fit into me, his balls are slapping at me.

"Tlezus! I'm dying!"

He laughs and only moves quicker and quicker. "Oh, come on my cock, scream like the little slut you are."

"Yes!" An orgasm swarms through me. My body tenses up to take the blow before I fall to pieces. He has messed up my insides, and he is still good to keep going with that large strong cock.

He pulls from me when I need him and crave how much he can stretch me.

"Tle— Argh!" I scream when he slams all the way back into me. When it feels like it can't get any better, his tail thrusts into me, making his cock in my pussy feel even larger.

I moan some more. There are tears dropping from me. His tail and his cock work together, throwing me up to a high followed by more highs.

"I love you, Tlezus!"

"Me? Or which part of me?"

I wrap my arms around his muscular body, crashing my lips against his.

"All of you. You, your cock, your tail. All of you!"

He keeps doing things to me; he's making me his fucktoy and I fucking love every moment of this. His cock is just perfect for me.

"You are such a naughty and dirty slut, with a pussy that begs to get pounded all the time."

"Yes, I'm naughty, punish me, Tlezus!"

He goes on and on with me. The pleasure is so strong that I might die. So much so that the surroundings blurs, leaving only his cock and his tail fucking my holes, using me however he wants.

"My mate, my slutty mate. Astrid..."

I gasp. I murmur something, but I can't even make out words now.

His cock twitches and swells inside me, stretching me even more than before. He's going to come inside me now.

He kisses me again while he picks up speed, as if that's even possible. His tongue swirls against my insides, sending another flame through my body. He's using all holes possible, even my mouth, and this is fucking amazing.

"Mine now, my mate. I'm keeping you, and you aren't going anywhere."

"Yes!" I moan against his lips.

His cock twitches and his hot cum shoots into the deepest part of me.

He fills me within seconds, so much that his cum would have dripped out of me had his cock wasn't there blocking the path.

Maybe this is the way baekexes fill up their mate with their cum, making the heat so strong. I'll never forget about this.

He grunts, stopping as he catches his breath. His cock is still inside me, almost a plug from letting his cum spill.

"Astrid... I love you."

"I think I've told you a lot of times now. I love you, Tlezus."

"More times than I've made you come?"

I smack his chest, but I am so exhausted that I won't even tickle him. "Maybe, who knows?"

He smirks and pecks a kiss on my cheek. "Then I will make sure to fix that."

He pulls from me. I can finally breathe. Maybe this is going to be my everyday, now. He won't stop wanting me, can't say I can stop, either.

"You can take a break for now. We'll get back to it in a moment."

What?

He laughs as he strokes my cheek. "Don't worry, I will take care of you in more ways than you can imagine."

And I don't doubt him. With how hard his cock still is, this is going to be a long night that I will love a bit too much, with my mate, who I can't love enough.

Chapter 15

Tlezus

It's another dawn, another day of being in the spaceship with my crew. It almost feels the same as it has always been. I sit in my chair in the command center and stare at the map ahead, resting my elbow on the armrest and my head on my hand. We are away from Vammos now, supplies and everything have been stocked, the crew had their fun, and all is good.

The crew is busy monitoring everything about the ship and outside of the ship. They are quiet though, there aren't even noises of typing or tapping. Nothing is happening, which is often better than when something is happening.

I blink while I stare at the screen for a moment longer. It's getting boring when there's nothing interesting to do here. No target for us to hit, no new intelligence from the Empire cracked or received.

What's Astrid doing in my room? Now that she's my mate, I don't have to worry about her trying to sneak out of the ship or do something stupid just so she thinks she can escape from me.

She's not one of the crew, so she isn't here with me. It's boring here with nothing to do.

Urkaits is by my side, standing, also staring ahead, maybe staring blankly like I am.

"Captain."

"Yes?"

"Can I have a few words with you? In private?"

"Sure." I don't like the sound of that. Maybe I already know what he has to say. If he's still planning to make me let Astrid go or take her away from me, I will have no end with him.

I stand and head to the strategic center, which is the closest place without any other beings. I open the door with my tail and flick the lights with my hand. "What do you have to tell me?"

Urkaits turns and makes sure the door is closed before he clears his throat. "Astrid..."

Yes, I guessed it. "What's about her? Maybe I haven't made it clear enough earlier. She's staying here with me now."

"As what?" He has a deep frown on his face. Maybe he's worrying about something I haven't thought of.

"Huh?"

"I mean, who is she, and how we should regard her? Do you want her to warm your bed? Are you keeping a pleasure worker for yourself? Taking her as your mate?"

I blink. There are some differences between those. "As my mate. She's not going anywhere away from me."

The tension in him eases. "If that's the case, good to know. I will let everyone know and get them to behave accordingly."

"They asked you about her?"

He smirks. "Yes, quite a few did. They wonder whether you want to keep a pleasure worker on the ship and... when you will get bored with her."

A fire bursts inside me. I'm never going to be bored with Astrid, and—

He says, "If they know she's your mate now, they will stop thinking about that."

Ah... "Sure, I understand the curiosity. She's mine and mine alone."

"Yes, I understand, Captain." He bows his head and I understand where the question comes from. He says, "On that word, congrats. I've been wanting to ask that myself too. Not whether you'll get bored with her, but whether you are taking her as your mate."

"What do you mean?"

"Captain, you and I have spent almost our whole lives training and growing up together. I know it from the way you look at her. I just didn't know whether that was a question I should ask."

I take an abrupt breath. I didn't give that much thought. "How do you see... me taking a human female as my mate?" I'm the leader of my fleet, so I should be a good model for the rest of my crew.

He shrugs. "I don't see any issue with that. I'm happy for you. It's not that easy to find a mate in this vast universe. I haven't met mine, though I'm not sure whether having a mate is in my plan. I don't see myself having one."

I also have never seen myself having a mate, but when I met Astrid, I just knew.

Urkaits says, "But I think you know, most baekexes will land and establish their lives with their mates on some planet."

I know... but I'm not leaving my fleet. "I've devoted my life to fighting the Empire, successful or not."

His tail dances. "I mean, that's no rules saying you have to, but that's a bit more common. Just like how when we were teenagers, we get into training, and when we're adults, we board a ship. Not every single baekex does that, but a lot do."

"I will think about that." I don't want to leave my fleet.

But maybe I should ask Astrid what she wants. Just like when I asked her yesterday, we should try to make it work, but we want different things. I have no idea.

"Urkaits, go look over them for now. I will consider what to do next."

"Sure, Captain."

I get out of the room, heading to my own. The guards on the way nod when I walk past them. Maybe Urkaits wants me to retire from my life on the ship. If I leave, he will get the crew. It will be approved by the Fleet. Urkaits is experienced and knows what he's doing. He's also the one I will trust my crew to if it comes down to that.

Why is my room so far away? I don't remember it taking so long for me to reach there.

I miss Astrid, even though I'm not away from her for long. I forgot, maybe I've been away for an hour? Not very long, but it feels like ages.

At my door, I open it and go inside. She looks up from bed and grins. She has been laying on my bed on her stomach, watching something on the tablet I gave her.

"Barney! You're done with work now?" She stands on the bed and hugs me, which puts her a bit taller than me. Not bad when I can bury my face in her boobs. She has some soft ones, good to be my pillow.

She strokes my hair and pecks a kiss on my forehead, something she can't usually do unless we are laying in bed. "How are we doing now? Are you bored?"

I glance at the screen. It's still on and she's watching a video. "What's that?"

"Oh, it's Barney and Friends. Super super old show. Watched it when I was very young with my parents, somehow it showed up on re-air."

"Huh?" Is that where Barney comes from?

She picks up the tablet and gestures for me to sit by her side. "This."

There are a few cartoon dinosaur figures on the screen with a few human kids. There's one... that's purple with some silly green spots on his back. "That's Barney."

She nods and leans into me. "Yes, isn't he cute?"

I take a breath and grunt. "And what about this kids' show makes you think about me? Just because this thing is purple?"

She blinks with those innocent cute eyes that make it a bit too hard to be mad at. "Yes? And you are nice to me, like this Barney."

"And this is what you called a purple dino."

"Yes, don't you think that's pretty accurate? And just like you?" She rubs my stomach. "You are purple like this one, though you don't have the green spots and the tail is different."

I hiss. "I thought it was one of those dinosaurs I've watched in human movies."

"Oh, which?"

"Um... Jurassic World? Like, those large and formidable ones. It's also an old movie, and..."

She busts out laughing so hard that she falls on the bed, almost flipping over. "You are so cute, Barney."

I grunt. "Had I known Barney was this silly purple thing, I'd never have let you call me that."

"Oh, Barney, you can't use at least some cuteness in your life? I mean, you can be one of those super strong monsters for sure."

This woman is so insufferable. Why did I even want her as a mate? "Come on, you can't do this to me. I'm a bandit, I'm supposed to be threatening, not fluffy like this thing."

I point at the screen, while the Barney dino and the yellow dino are dancing with two kids with silly plastic food in their hands. I grimace as heat burns my cheek. This is just silly. Why did I even find that cute for a moment when she first mentioned that...?

"Astrid... tell me you didn't think of me as that silly cartoon when you first met me."

She laughs again, burning my cheeks even harder. She must think I'm a joke.

She squeezes my hand. "No, come on, I know you're a scary warrior. And like I told you, I only thought of Barney when you made me call you something else when we were at the space station. You have yourself to blame."

I growl. She's so annoying. "And? You kept calling me that."

"Yes. Now you aren't the scary monster to me, not like those big dinos that want to eat me alive."

My heart flutters. I sigh. Maybe I can't get mad at her as easily as I should. She's... a bit too cute, a bit...

"I'm going to punish you for calling me Barney."

"Oh..." She grins. "I know I'm going to be tortured so hard that I'll want more of that."

This crazy woman. Why is this setting me on fire? I want to hold her in my arms and... do all the things to her and make her beg and scream for forgiveness.

Chapter 16

Astrid

Ouch... Maybe I shouldn't have teased my Barney like that. Tlezus will never forgive me. I'm on the bed now, staring at the ceiling, too exhausted to even move an inch. He always makes me a useless pile.

Maybe he won't have to worry about me fleeing places since he took me as his mate. He could just fuck me hard enough and I will be useless for a long time.

Tlezus hisses. "Are you still going to call me Barney now?"

I barely lift my finger, pointing to the ceiling. "If that's going to turn you on, I'll definitely keep calling you that— Ouch!"

He spanks my clit with his tail. "You are so annoying, so insufferable."

"You're smiling," I guess because I can't see his face from here.

"No, I'm not."

"Your voice outed you, Barney."

He grunts. Maybe I was right all along.

I reach my toes to his knee, the only way I can reach him with my tired body, since he is probably sitting and watching me, also on the bed. "You secretly like the name Barney a bit too much. Who are you fooling?"

He groans, but he clears his throat. "All the joking and fucking aside, I have something to ask you." His tail wraps around my waist and nudges me to get up.

I push against the bed, but even with the help of his tail, all I manage is to lean onto the other side and onto his lap instead. "Yes, what do you want to talk about?"

"I'm a bandit. You want to run an inn."

Ah... Right... We still have to figure that part out.

He strokes my hair. His tail remains wrapped around me. "What do you want? I want to stay here with my fleet, but you're my mate now. I want you to be happy too."

I blink and start stroking the tip of his tail because it keeps moving in front of me. "I mean, it would be great if I could run an inn or something. But... I think now that the inn is pretty much destroyed by that attack, it may finally be the time for me to uproot myself and look for a better place to rebuild it. I still have the blueprint of the inn; I can build it again on some other planet. The problem is just..."

"I'll pay for all of that."

My breath halts and I almost jump from my bed. "Are you sure? Do you even know how much that will cost?"

He shrugs. "Don't care as long as you're happy."

I squint at him. While I appreciate that, I don't like false hope and I hate to waste anyone's time.

He chuckles. "You have the insurance money, and I have my own savings from my years of flights. Not to mention, the Fleet may give us some funding. Baekexes could use a place where we can take a break from the chaos of flying, and we a place friendly to us would be nice. We just have to find the right planet."

"And we can do that in the middle of the Empire's region, just to piss them off."

He laughs. "I like the sound of that, but no, that's too risk. We will start it somewhere else. Wait, now that I think about it, if we can get the Fleet on board, we can set up inns or outposts on different planets, then you can be with me most of the time while we travel and you will get to run all the inns."

I stare at him. "Barney, are you a bit crazy after I called you Barney?"

He scowls. "What do you mean? I'm very serious. We can figure out a way for us to be together. My fleet can take on some other tasks other than going into the Empire's region. We can patrol and hit the Empire's ships from within the Alliance's region. Or, if you're worried about space battles, you can stay on a planet and wait for me. I have no problem bringing back shiny loot for my mate."

My heart hammers in my chest and my hands are so cold that they could turn water into ice. Is he certain about that? I can travel with him, visit lots of planets, and run more than one inn now? "Tell me I'm not dreaming."

"What is it that you humans do? I should pinch you?"

"That'll work— Ouch!"

Of all places, he pinches my nipples.

"Is this working? Are you dreaming?"

I smack his chest. All he does is laugh. "Fine, I'm still seeing my Barney, so I think I'm not dreaming. Though I didn't imagine you pinching my nipple."

He pecks a kiss on my cheek. "I'm never what you imagined, always better."

Maybe he isn't wrong. "So, what are we going to do now?"

"I'll talk to the Fleet and they will decide whether they like the plan. If they reject it, we can come up with something else."

Epilogue

Astrid

"Hello, how can I help you?" I nod to the being that arrives at the inn. He's a daecolus male, tall and thin with ram-like horns on his head.

"My group wants three bedrooms."

"Sure." I type in his information, count out the coins, and pick up the key cards he will need from the system. I hand him his cards. "Here you go! Once you get to the third floor, turn left; it's close to the lift."

"Thank you." He walks away, going to the table with his friends.

I take a deep breath. There is a tasty smell of sausages and bacon in the air. I sit on the stool behind the counter as I watch beings drinking and having fun.

Keeyna has two trays with him and a lot of snacks on those plates. He ducks and twists around to avoid bumping into other patrons while trying his best to not drop the snacks.

I have more employees now, and more patrons than I've ever seen.

Luekotz is busy in the kitchen. We got him a few trainees so that it will be feasible to serve everyone. But maybe those newer beings are giving him a hard time. He isn't the best at teaching others, and not the best at talking.

If my parents were here, they would be proud of me, hopefully.

"Astrid."

"Hello? Oh! Nelutho, Kimberly." I smile, even though part of me still... feels sorry that I didn't leave with them after they spent so much effort looking for me. "Didn't expect to see you here."

Kimberly smiles. "We've been hearing stories about here for some time now. But we've been busy on the other side. Now, we've finally got a chance to visit. Looks like the business is doing amazing."

"Oh... You can say that." Will they not like how this place is started up by the baekex fleet's money? "It took a bit to get it running."

Nelutho nods. "Baekex."

Kimberly says, "He's asking whether this place was set up with them in mind."

"You could say that. I guess you kind of guessed that when I decided not to go with you."

Nelutho nodded. "Surprised."

I say, "He treats me well, even though we didn't start smoothly."

Kimberly looks at Nelutho and she grins, sweetly. "We understand that sometimes, finding a mate can be very interesting."

Nelutho rolls his eyes; maybe he isn't the type that likes to talk about himself, or he doesn't like talking no matter what the topic is.

Kimberly is about to say something when there's a growl from the door, coming close quickly. The two of them turn around, and I also look over there. Someone is already drunk this early in the day?

"What are you doing here?" Tlezus hisses at Nelutho.

Kimberly laughs. "Don't worry, we're just regular patrons, if your inn will serve us."

Tlezus watches them. "Really? You're not planning something fishy?"

Nelutho huffs. "In the public? I strike, no hint."

I gesture for Tlezus to come to my side of the counter instead. Hopefully, he remembers that there are other patrons around and he shouldn't fight Nelutho here, especially when Nelutho isn't planning anything bad and he isn't trying to hurt me.

Tlezus comes over within a blink and he pulls me close to him. "Nelutho. I've heard your name for quite some time now, and we almost met. You tried to take my mate away from me."

Kimberly says, "To be accurate, she wasn't your mate back then. And we didn't take her away. We were commissioned to bring her back to her home planet."

Nelutho adds, "No money."

Kimberly nods. "Yes, and that. We just wanted to help her when some baekex took her away against her will."

There's tension in Tlezus. I rub his side. "You weren't wrong, but he and I are good now. Sometimes, it's just hard to know someone without meeting them and talking to them. I think in front of the Empire, we are not enemies."

Nelutho nods. "The Empire... that's why we're here."

Kimberly says, "If we get caught by the Empire, we will also have it bad, maybe no better than baekexes. I'm happy for the two of you. I mean, if Astrid didn't like it here, we were going to take her with us and go back to Edezon, but she's happy here."

I nod. "Yes, I am. Thank you for looking out for me."

Tlezus groans. "Maybe the two of you should just get a seat and entertain yourselves."

Nelutho puts his card on the counter with a low thud. "Three rooms, six of us."

I take his card. "Sure. Thanks for your business, both back there and here."

Tlezus says, "Yes, that. More importantly, have you heard about the strange movement of the Empire's outpost? The one furthest away from the Alliance."

Nelutho's eyes light up. "Yes. Baekexes."

"You think that it was caused by our fleet?"

"Probably."

The two of them go on talking about that now. Maybe that's an advantage for the Fleet, since the inn is great for collecting information and for them to plan attacks. It's starting to become a gathering point for beings that don't fit into other places.

Kimberly rolls his eyes. "Look at these males. A moment ago, they are ready to fight, but the next moment, they are so interested in talking to each other."

"Do you guys want to beat the Empire? Like Tlezus and the Fleet?"

Kimberly shakes her head. "No, that's not what we do. We're bounty hunters, as you know. We travel a lot. In theory, our proper job is to discover new planets and markets for Nelutho's family business to expand to. But you know him... he doesn't care about doing that. We trade when we don't have a task, or say, we just do whatever interests him. Just like trying to help you. No one paid us, but we still did it, just trying to do the right thing."

"That's interesting. And to be honest, past me never saw myself with this inn and a few others that I also run." Now that there are a few for me to manage and look over, I fly a lot more than I used to.

"I never saw myself traveling with Nelutho and his team either, Sometimes, things just happen."

Nelutho tugs on Kimberly's elbow; maybe they are ready to join their crew now.

Tlezus cups my face in his hands after they leave. "Astrid, did you miss me?"

"Barney, you say that as if you've been gone for long."

"I was gone a whole week, it's quite a long time."

Warmth swells inside me. "So you are the one who missed me."

"Oh..." He grins. "I guess so." He leans to my ear and whispers, "I missed your tight pussy and your moans."

My cheeks burn and I smack his shoulder, only for him to wrap his arms around me, including my arms, and I can't smack him some more.

"Dirty Tlezus."

"You just love me."

"I do. How was the trip though? Other than getting us fresh stock and not needing the shipment companies."

"The Fleet is happy, but now you'll have to go to another planet with me."

"They want to start even more?" That was a lot quicker than I expected.

"They trust you."

I take a breath. There's a stir in my stomach, growing so much that I want to puke. "But I don't trust myself that much. I think it's crazy enough they even let me borrow the money to start up here. You know, my inn back on Edezon wasn't very successful."

He gestures at the patrons busy eating at the tables, the ones waiting at the lift and the few at the other counter checking in with my assistant, who will be in charge of this place when I'm not around.

"Look at all of them. You set up this place and you hired these beings. Your old inn wasn't doing great because the location was bad. You are good enough to run these places, and you can run more."

I let out a breath, though the ache is still there in my stomach. "Maybe? I don't know."

"It's just like when I lead my fleet. You will never feel ready."

Maybe? I suppose when he leads his crew, when everyone's life is in his hands, that's scarier.

He pecks a kiss on my cheek. "We will do amazingly well."

"I still don't know about that."

"You have me, so everything will be fine."

"You are the reason nothing is ever fine, Barney. Do you remember the many times we've tried to discuss important issues? What have those become?"

He gulps and his tail sneaks its way to run my inner thigh again. "You can't blame me when I can't always have you here with me."

"Excuses, excuses."

Tlezus has shifted his focus a bit, turning to collecting intelligence for the Fleet. That means less fighting and less risk for him, and more time to spend with me. His fleet also shrank since he doesn't need that many hands and tails; also naturally since most of his warriors want to fight the Empire, not run around starting businesses.

"Barney, I want to tell you something."

He frowns. "What? I hope it's something good."

I kiss him. "It must be tough giving up what you love and devoted yourself to."

He covers my hand with his. "I didn't give it up. I swore my life to stopping the Empire and fighting to take back the baekexes' planet. I'm still doing that, just differently. And I can be with you. That's a win. Also because of you, now, Nelutho talks to us baekexes. I'm not sure whether he wants to have a relationship with us, but at least we probably won't fight."

That's not bad. Tlezus mentioned that because of his way of life, he has limited friends. If he can find someone he can at least do some small talk with, that's a good thing. "That's nice. I don't think I told you before, but you probably could have guessed when you found his number in my pocket, but the day before you arrived at my inn, he was there warning me about a purple male with a tail and his fleet of bandits."

He laughs. "I guess so. He loves sticking his horns in where they don't belong. He's pretty famous for that, actually."

"They aren't bad beings."

"They don't plan against us, and that's all that matters."

"Oh..." I guess he isn't wrong. I hadn't thought about it in that light.

He hugs me again. "I think you should call it a night now. You have something more important to do."

I rub his tail briefly, then stop before the others can see. "About what?"

"To be with your mate."

Or say, to be fucked again and again.

"Sure, my Barney, I love you."

"Astrid... I love you too."

Get a bonus story!

https://icepawpress.com/alina-riley

He doesn't even know what's an Easter Bunny but he hates my event before I can even host it...

This grumpy and annoying grey alien with a tail hates me the moment I show up at the doorstep of the community center. For him, any celebration is stupid. Except I'm going to host the party for the kids and I'm going to do it amazingly well. He won't get to stand in my way. Everything is going great until... my partner for the event falls sick... Now, I need someone to help me with the bunny costume...

Also By Alina Riley

A Mate For The Luraella Traders
Saved by The Alien Boss
Guarded by The Alien Boss
Rescued by The Alien Boss
The Alien Boss's Hook Up

Crashing into an Alien Tribe
Trapped by Snow
Caught by Fire
Stranded by Vine

Mated to the Baekex Bandit
Taken by The Alien Bandit
Saved by the Alien Bandit
Healing the Alien Bandit

Mated to the Zalcor Rebels
The Space Outlaw's Treasure

Also From Ice Paw Press

Dark and Steamy Paranormal Romance
The Wolf's Captive: Collateral

Urban Fantasy
The Hidden Order of Magic: Shaken
The Magic Rebel

Steamy Sci-Fi Romance
A Mate For The Luraella Traders
Crashing into an Alien Tribe
Mated to the Baekex Bandit

Dark Mafia Romance
Kneel to the Jarockis

www.ingramcontent.com/pod-product-compliance
Lightning Source LLC
Chambersburg PA
CBHW031144130726
47988CB00006B/2526